Dead of Winter: A Ransom & Fortune Adventure

Volume 2

Michelle Miles

DEAD OF WINTER: A RANSOM & FORTUNE ADVENTURE

Cover Design by Erin Dameron-Hill

ISBN: 978-1-7343068-4-2

Dead of Winter

A Ransom & Fortune Adventure, Volume 2
This title was previously published as part two of A Bend in Time.

At the mercy of a faulty time machine, Skye Ransom and Dane Fortune are forced to randomly leap through time on a wild, roller-coaster ride of danger as they try to get back to the 21st century. Each jump sends them farther away from home but brings them closer together in a bond that not even a time bender can sever.

With their last time leap, they end up in a strange futuristic frigid world with two opposing tribes. The arrival of the time travelers sets into motion a long-dead prophecy indicating Skye is the future of one of the tribes, causing a rebellion. When one of the tribe leaders kidnaps Skye intent on marrying her and sacrificing her to the gods to help him win that rebellion, Dane uses his military tactics to launch an all-out war to save her before she's burned alive on a funeral pyre. But will he be able to save her before it's too late?

Prologue

Present Day, Arlington, VA, six months after Skye and Dane time travel to Scotland

Archimedes—or Ark as he preferred—sat in the interrogation room with only a pack of cigarettes to keep him company. The overhead light emitted an incessant buzzing, the glare from it pooling on the metal table in front of him. His wrists were still cuffed and the only movement he had was to take a puff from the cigarette every now and again.

He'd been sitting in the metal chair, alone in the room for some time. The last person he'd seen ripped the black hood off his head before departing through the only door. There wasn't even a two-way mirror to give him the suggestion others were watching him.

But he was no idiot. He knew they were watching. He assumed there was a camera somewhere in the ceiling tiles overhead. They would not let someone like Ark Crane sit alone for hours without being watched.

So, he waited. Smoked his cigarette, crushed it out. Lit another. Smoke from his last one curled in lazy circles upward. He was a patient man, though. He could outwait whoever his captors were.

At last, the door opened, and a tall silver haired man entered. His face was a roadmap of wrinkles and wise blue eyes. He carried a thick folder which he tossed on the table and then took the empty chair opposite Ark. He pulled a pen out of his pocket then flipped open the folder which had a crude headshot of Ark stapled to a stack of thick papers.

A case file, no doubt.

The man gave a smile that didn't reach his eyes and waited as Ark crushed out his last cigarette.

"Mr. Crane, I trust you have been treated well." He spoke in a clipped British accent, his voice gravely as though he'd finally managed to quit his bad habit of two packs a day.

"Well?" He snorted. "I've been sitting in this fucking room for hours." He shifted in the metal chair to prove his point.

The smile didn't leave the man's face as he glanced down at the empty packet of cigarettes. "Camels. I used to smoke those myself."

Ark shoved aside the ash tray and leaned toward the man. "Who the fuck are you and what the fuck do you want with me?"

There was a pause, still that cold smile, "I'm Charles Ridgewood. Tell me what you know about Skye Ransom."

Ark sat back in his chair, the memory of the woman he'd been hired to kill floating through his mind. As the daughter of the deceased William Ransom, she was heiress to his billion-dollar fortune. She was a tall, athletic, smart, college girl with hair the color of a shiny new penny and striking indigo eyes. Killing her would have giving him the cash he needed to get to Belize.

"Why?" he asked, his tone suspicious.

"You were hired by Conner Dade to kill her, correct?"

"I was." If he knew, then why ask?

"That was after you killed her parents, William and Emily?"

"Conner wanted them all dead."

"Yes, I'm aware. What else do you know about her?"

His brows knit. "I'm not sure what information you want out of me about the girl."

"When was the last time you saw her?" He answered with another question.

The memory of that day in downtown Arlington came crashing back. He'd followed her and the man who had proclaimed himself her bodyguard in the small specialty store.

If you want her, you'll have to go through me, the man said, as though issuing a challenge.

There had been a scuffle between the two of them. When the poor shopkeeper got in the way, Ark shot him. He'd crashed through the dressing room to get to the girl, but her bodyguard shoved him backward. The next thing he knew, they both disappeared in the oddest lightning storm he'd ever seen leaving behind nothing but charred remains of the dressing room.

It'd thrown him backward and he'd crashed through racks of clothing before coming to a halt on the floor. With the dead shopkeeper and the burned walls and floor, he knew he had to make a hasty exit before the cops showed up.

"Several months ago."

Ridgewood clicked the pen and scratched notes on a paper in the folder. "And where was it you saw her?"

He watched as the man's pen hovered over the paper, waiting for an answer. "A specialty clothing store in downtown Arlington. What is it you want to know?"

Ridgewood scribbled more notes, then clicked off the pen. He dropped it on the folder and sat back, meeting his gaze. "That specialty clothing store was a costume shop. The owner was found dead. Shot in the head. Know anything about that?"

"Does it matter if I do?" he countered.

Ridgewood smiled as though he already knew the answer. "Was Skye Ransom alone when you last saw her?"

"No, there was a man with her."

"Who?"

"How should I know?"

"I think you *do* know, Mr. Crane." He slipped a photo out from the back of the folder and pushed it toward him. It was a picture of the girl's bodyguard. "Was it this man?"

The picture of the dark-haired man had been taken when he was unaware. As though he'd been followed by someone. Much like Ark had been followed. As soon as he realized someone was tracking him, he'd tried to go into hiding. Get out of the States. But they'd caught him. Like an idiot, he'd allowed himself to be captured.

"Yes."

"This is Dane Fortune. He's former Army Ranger and Secret Service. Hired by William Ransom as executive protection, only you managed to kill him and his wife anyway. We believe he's protecting the girl."

Ark nodded agreement. "This is all real interesting but what is your point in all this?"

Ridgewood laced his fingers and rested his hands on the table in front of him as he leaned forward. "Have you heard of Janus Force?"

He shook his head.

"Ah, good. I hoped you hadn't." Without elaborating, Ridgewood flipped up his headshot and skimmed the page beneath it. "Former Navy SEAL turned hit man. I find that an interesting transition. Would you like to tell me about that?"

"No," Ark said.

He chuckled. "No matter. I already know all about you."

So why ask the question? To see how cooperative he'd be?

Ridgewood closed the file and laced his fingers again. "Janus Force was created as a black ops division of the NSA in conjunction with DARPA and we've recruited you."

Ark's eyes narrowed. "To do what?"

"To work for us tracking down two people who have the prototype of a machine we'd like to get back."

The back of his neck tingled. "Who?"

"Dane Fortune and Skye Ransom. We call it Operation Chronos and you'll be an integral part of it."

So that was it, then. Why he was asking all the questions about the two of them. "I haven't agreed to do it."

"Oh, you have." Ridgewood gave a sharp nod of his head, his tone brooking no argument. "Because if you say no, I have men waiting outside to kill you now. The world will not mourn the loss of someone like you, Mr. Crane. Trust me on this. My suggestion is you take those skills you've acquired over the years as both a hit man and Navy SEAL and track down these two before they cause irreparable damage."

"Irreparable damage to the machine?"

Ridgewood nodded. "And time. You see, the prototype they have is a time machine. William Ransom called it a time bender. It's the very machine Connor Dade wanted to get his hands on when he hired you. That's *why* he hired you. Or did you not know that?"

Ark stared at the man, his gut twisting into a tight knot. No, he'd had no idea why Conner hired him other than he wanted the entire Ransom family taken out.

"We managed to recover the stolen notes and journals from Dade when we took him into custody."

"You have him in custody?" Ark couldn't hide the surprise in his voice.

"Indeed. Several months ago. He knew the value of cooperation. Do you?"

Ridgewood's calm demeanor chilled Ark to the marrow of his bones. He realized with some dismay he was already in deep. So deep he wouldn't be able to crawl his way out of it. He glanced at the door, wondering if Ridgewood was telling the truth.

Without a word, the man rose, walked to the door, opened it. Two armed men stood on the other side. Men in suits. Men who would do exactly what Ridgewood said without question.

"All I have to do is give them the word, Mr. Crane, and your life ends. The choice is yours. Do you agree to help us?"

Live and track down Dane and Skye or die right here, right now. Not exactly options he relished. Finally, Ark nodded. Ridgewood closed the door and returned to his seat opposite him.

"Good. Now, the two used the time bender some time ago, so it has taken some doing to track them down. However, with the help of Mr. Dade and another scientist who understands the space-time continuum, we were able to get a second prototype up and running. You'll be using that one to go after them."

Ark's mouth went dry as he stared at the man. Suddenly, his nicotine craving increased tenfold. He reached for the pack, remembered it was empty, then shoved it away.

"You want me to do what?"

"You'll go after them with the second time bender. Don't worry. It's quite safe." He smiled again and somehow Ark wasn't sure he believed him. "We have their location and are ready to launch the operation as quickly as possible."

Knowing he didn't have a choice, Ark gave the man an affirmative nod. "Then I better pack my bags."

Somewhere in Rural Pennsylvania

It had been six months since Skye and Dane disappeared. Six months since he could get his computers back up and running. Six months of zero contact with anyone at the lab. Thomas Hardy had never abandoned a job before in his life.

He was the straight-laced, always follow the rules kind of guy. He was not the going-underground-hiding-out-to-save-your-life kind of guy.

But it's what he had to do when he found out the extent of the involvement Conner Dade had with DARPA and the NSA and some secret organization called Janus Force. He'd been using every internet café he could since leaving Virginia, so he could research Janus Force.

When he discovered they were a covert division with their fingers in both the NSA and DARPA, he knew they were in some serious shit. When he really thought about the name— Janus—he realized their intent was to get their hands on the time bender. What better thing to name a covert black ops division than after the god of beginnings and endings, gates and time?

He'd heard the term the last day he showed up for work at Goldenrod Research Technology. When he realized Lucy had turned to the dark side. When Conner had been taken into custody. It'd taken him a while to put the pieces together, but he figured out they were the ones who tried to take them all out at the old tech building the day Skye and Dane time traveled. Lucy and Conner were now working for them, too. It would be only a matter of time before they recruited him.

He packed up what equipment he could and got out of town as fast as possible. He tried to pick the most remote place he could think of that had secure internet. He thought of going to his family home and setting up shop in his dad's basement, but he didn't want to put his father's life in danger. He ended up at an abandoned farmhouse in Amish country.

It had taken him months to get his computer system up and running but he was finally ready to log in and see if he could track down Skye and Dane.

As soon as he booted up and launched the tracking software, the blip on the screen indicated a time bender located in present day Arlington, Virginia. He knew that couldn't be right. If they'd made it back, he'd for sure know about it. Maybe his algorithms were off? Or maybe they really did make it back?

Suddenly, a second blip came on the screen. He tapped the keyboard, bringing up the information on it and realized it was a place in Russia in the year 2334. His eyes immediately went back to the first blip in the present day, Arlington, Virginia.

It could only mean one thing—they'd built another time bender. As he watched, the blip began a rapid blink, indicating it had been used. It went dark and then second later came back on. The location was Russia, 2334.

"Oh, shit."

Chapter 1
An Icy Reception

The last thing Dane Fortune remembered was Skye pushing the button on the time bender and then a maelstrom of lightning surrounding them and then a fall through time and space. It had been a swirling kaleidoscope of colors as time bent around them creating circle after circle.

Skye passed out quickly. He couldn't hold onto her, much as he wanted. She was ripped away from him with such violence, he nearly lost a limb. And then suddenly there was nothing at all.

He awoke to the throbbing pain of his ankle still trying to heal and the sound of a woman whimpering. A cold numbness settled into his bones. It took several moments before he realized the woman was Skye and they had landed in some type of arctic climate.

The blinding brightness was a snowy embankment. A brilliant sun centered in an azure sky and in the distance, he could see serene sapphire waters with ice floes floating along as though they had long been a part of the landscape.

Dane dragged himself to Skye's side. Horror struck him as he realized a jagged ice-covered rock had ripped open her shoulder. Blood seeped from the wound, staining the snow bright red.

"Skye, can you hear me?"

She whimpered again. Her teeth chattered. "Hurts."

"I know. Looks bad. You need stitches, I think," he said.

"Dane…it's so c-cold."

"Yeah, we need to find some shelter and warmer clothes. Any idea where we are?"

She shook her head. "Not a clue."

He looked around trying to figure out their surroundings, and then glanced back at her. She wavered as dizziness swept over her. "Skye, you're pale. Don't pass out."

He wrapped his arm around her waist and lifted her to her feet. "Put your arm around my shoulders."

"I don't want to walk anywhere. I'm tired."

"I know you are, but we can't stay here. We'll freeze to death."

She leaned all her weight into him. They hobbled together across the icy ground.

"I'll figure out something, build a fire, get you warm. If I don't, you're going to go into shock."

Ahead, he could see three people walking towards them cresting a ridgeline. They all wore heavy furs, making them seem mammoth in size. They even wore fur-lined boots, with fur trimming the tops. The one in the middle carried a spear.

"Hey!" Dane called.

He hoped they landed someplace where they spoke English.

The three stopped, not moving for what seemed an eternity while Dane continued to limp toward them, laboring with Skye's weight. Her head rolled on her shoulders.

"Skye, stay awake," he urged. To the trio, he shouted, "You there! I need some help."

They spoke rapidly, softly between them and Dane could hear nothing but the murmur of voices on the chilly wind. He watched as the one in the middle with the spear came forward while the others waited. He was a tall man, with dark hair and a long scraggly beard. His eyes were large and round and dark as coal. Dane couldn't determine his body shape under the heavy animal skins he wore as protection from the elements. He paused in front of him, looking him up and down with a wary eye.

"You are a stranger here," he said, showing yellowed teeth. He spoke English, but his words were clipped, his voice hinted at a strange accent.

"I am," Dane said. "My companion is hurt. We need your help."

The tall man's eyes shifted to Skye, roving over her as though she was fair game. Dane didn't like the lascivious look he gave her. His gaze paused longer than it should have on her round breasts. Dane shook her, hoping she'd wake up, but she was out.

"Listen, she's in shock. She has a gash in her shoulder and she's bleeding. I need to get her inside. You know, someplace warm," Dane said. "Now."

"I will take you to the camp." The man's dark gaze flickered back to Dane. "The chieftain will want to see you."

"Fine, whatever."

"I will carry your companion," the man said, licking his lips and reaching for Skye.

"No," Dane snapped, clutching her tighter against him. "She's fine. I'll take her."

The man paused in mid-reach, his dark cold eyes riveted to Dane's face. He dropped his arms, gave him a slight nod. "As you wish."

He started back toward his two tribemates. Dane followed. His arms ached from carrying Skye as he favored his sore ankle. His good one was getting quite a workout and burned with pain. Despite the cold, sweat rolled down the side of his face, down his back.

It was a hard trek to the campsite down a snowy slope which was mostly ice. At the bottom, they turned eastward with the sun at their backs. He could hear Skye's shallow, rapid breathing in his ear, causing him to worry. Her condition was not good.

As they left the mountain behind, the snow melted away to dark brown grass. The campsite was nothing more than a half a dozen crude tents made from animal bones and skins set in a circle. There was a large bonfire in the center. Men and women stopped working to see what the hunters had brought back. They stared at them. The leader with the spear stopped, turned to Dane.

"Wait here."

He and the other two left Dane and Skye to stand and wait while they went to their camp. Spear-man conversed with a shorter version of himself, who fixed them with a withering stare. At last he nodded, turned and walked away, disappearing inside one of the tents. Spear-man returned to Dane.

"You and your companion will come with me."

They headed into the campsite and the spear-man took him into a tent. The bed was made of dried grass, furs, and animal skins. The man pointed to the bed.

"Put her there."

Gingerly, Dane laid Skye on the bed and covered her with the thick animal fur. Kneeling at her side, he checked her wound.

"Berta will attend her. You will come with me."

Dane looked up and saw a woman enter the tent. She had long, dark, unkempt hair, hollow eyes, and sunken cheeks. She wore the same animal skins as the man to cover her exposed skin. Dane stood, reluctant to leave.

"I want to make sure she's all right first," he said.

"No, you must come with me now. The chieftain will see you at once."

Left with no other choice, Dane followed him out of the tent and to the next one. Spear-man showed Dane inside, and then left. The chieftain was the short man he had seen earlier.

He sat cross-legged on the ground in front of a small fire. He smoked a crude pipe.

"Sit." The chieftain waved to the ground next to him.

As Dane sat on the ground, wincing as the movement pained his injured ankle, the heady scent of smoke filled the tent. Dane suspected there was more than mere tobacco in the pipe.

"I am Odren, leader of this clan. You are?"

"My name is Dane. My companion is Skye."

His brows drew together. He ran his hand over his chin, his skin bristling against the rough beard. "She is named for the heavens? How interesting. Tell me, stranger, what is your purpose here?"

"We are merely travelers. Just passing through," Dane said, trying to keep things simple.

"Winter is coming," the chieftain said. "And we are starving. You look as though you come from another clan, though I admit it is one I have not encountered before. Your dress is strange. Tell me, did you come to spy on us?"

Odren's gaze flickered over him. Dane could see how he thought he might dress strange. He had lost his jacket somewhere in Scotland. His white dress shirt was dirty, tattered and torn, missing buttons. His pants were in equally shabby shape and his ankle was still wrapped in the bandage. He ran his hand through his thick black hair.

"No," he answered simply. "As I said, we are merely travelers. My companion was injured when we…" He paused, unsure of his words. "When we fell into a crevasse."

"I see." Odren clamped the pipe between his lips, looking thoughtful. "I will be moving my camp southward soon. You are welcome to join us for the journey. However, we do not have much food. Our hunters have not been able to catch a reindeer in many weeks. Even fishing has not provided as much food as we'd like. My men were headed out to try again when they found you."

Dane said nothing as he pondered this. The men were fishing with spears? No wonder they couldn't catch much.

"You will no doubt want to return to your companion. I understand she was injured."

Dane nodded. "She was."

"Go then. You and your companion will be safe here with us. Far safer than with any other clan. We will find warmer clothes for you both and have them brought to you." He waved him away, his tone clipped and dismissive.

"Thank you."

As Dane rose and left the tent, he couldn't help but feel as though he had been shooed away.

~ ⧗ ~

The chieftain waited a moment until the stranger was gone and his best hunter returned.

"You look uneasy, Odren," the hunter said as he entered the tent and sat across from his chief.

"I am," Odren replied. "I do not like the looks of this stranger, Sovold." He extended the pipe to the younger man.

"What clan is he from?" Sovold took the offered pipe and inhaled.

"He is not from any clan we know, I think. His manner of dress is odd. He wears no furs."

"You think he's a threat?"

"I cannot be certain." He took the pipe back and clamped it between his teeth, taking a puff.

"His companion...the woman...she is unlike any I have ever seen. Her hair is the color of fire. She is...extraordinary."

"The stranger told me she is named for the heavens. She is called…" he paused, leaned forward to whisper the girl's name, "Skye."

"Skye? It is a sign then."

Odren nodded. "She is the one who could at last bring us what we most want."

"You intend to marry her then?" There was a slight edge or jealousy to Sovold's voice.

Odren chuckled. "You wish to have her as a mate, my friend?"

"I do," Sovold replied.

"Then you shall have her…*before* I marry her in the *troskian* ceremony."

Sovold gave a brief bow of his head to Odren. "You are too kind, my chief. However, I do not think her man will allow either of us to get close to her.

"Then perhaps we should make sure he does not get in our way," Odren replied with a crooked smile. "It would be a pity should he meet an unfortunate fate and the woman is left unprotected."

Sovold looked at him for a long moment and then smiled as well. "It would."

~ ⧗ ~

Dane returned to the tent with Skye and found her shivering and sweating under the heavy fur. The woman, Berta, knelt beside her, swabbing her wounds with a damp piece of cloth. Berta's dark gaze met his, her eyes wide and full of wonder.

"Your lady is ill," she said. "She has the fever."

Dane sat next to her, touched Skye's hand. Her skin was burning. "Will she be all right?"

"I do not know. Our shaman died last winter. We have no healer."

"Who are you then?" he asked.

"I am a midwife." She continued to cleanse the wound, then dipped the cloth in a bowl of water and wrung it out. "Sovold sent me here to look after her, but I can do nothing to help her."

"Sovold was the man who brought us here?" he asked.

"Yes, he is my mate. I carry his child even now." She patted her swelling belly. "But I fear bearing his child will kill me."

"Why is that?"

"His last mate died in childbirth and so did the child. The baby…" She paused, swallowed hard. Her face grew chalky and Dane could read her fear. "The baby was too big. It would not come out."

Dane sat back on his heels, horrified. They were so primitive they had no knowledge of the Cesarean section? The woman probably died needlessly. If they had been able to use the C-section, she and the child could have survived. Looking around at these dirty, haggard faces, though, told Dane he and Skye had dropped in the middle of some sort of Ice Age.

But when? One from the past, or something out of the future?

Berta reached for him, touched his sleeve at his torn cuff, breaking into his thoughts. Her fingers ran over the back of his hand then up his arm, sending a shiver through him. There was wonder in the primitive woman's eyes.

Her gaze searched his eyes and then her fingertips moved to his face, touching his scruffy cheeks and chin. He realized then she was fascinated by his almost-clean shaven state, that she probably had never seen an adult man without a beard or moustache. She gave him a small smile that didn't quite reach her hollowed eyes.

"Forgive me." She dropped her hand. "I have never seen a man like you."

"And you probably never will again," he said. "I'm…not from around here."

Her thick brows knit together in confusion. "Where do you come from, then?"

"A place far, far away," he replied. He shuddered as a cold wind whipped inside the small tent, making the opening flap.

"You are cold. I will gather warmer clothes for you." She uncurled her legs and rose to her full height.

"Odren said he would send some."

She paused at the door of the tent. "Our chieftain sometimes lies."

As she ducked out of the tent, a cold shiver ran up Dane's spine. It had nothing to do with the temperature either. What did that mean—he sometimes lied? Dane wasn't a trusting sort anyway, but that certainly planted the seed of doubt.

Skye moaned rolling her head from side to side.

He leaned over her, listening to her shallow breathing. Her eyes fluttered open then and she gave him a hollow look.

"Skye?"

Her arm came out from under the thick fur and he discovered she had shed the dress. Why he hadn't noticed that before when Berta was washing her wound, he didn't know. Her hand was fisted, reaching for him.

"Take it," she croaked.

She opened her blood-crusted fingers and the time bender fell out, landing on the fur next to her.

"Get out of here, Dane," she whispered, her voice hoarse. "I'm done."

"No, you're not," he insisted. "You'll be fine. All I need is something to sew you up."

"Oh, good. I haven't experienced enough excruciating pain in my life."

"Don't be sarcastic," he scolded. "I'm going to take care of you." He picked up the time bender and slipped it into his pocket.

"You intend to nurse me back to health, then?"

He scowled, readying a remark when she closed her eyes again, shivering under the heavy blankets. She reached for him and he grasped her hand.

"We didn't make it back. I'm s-sorry." She forced the words out through chattering teeth.

"Don't be. Thomas said he didn't think we could get back to where we started. Remember?" He didn't want to think about the alternate realities thing, but it crept into his thoughts anyway.

"Wh-what are we going to do?"

He squeezed her hand. "Keep going. It's all we can do."

"Where are w-we?"

"By my best estimate?" he asked. "I have no earthly idea."

Night came with the howling of the wind. Berta returned and as promised had warmer clothes with her. She even had a pair of animal skin boots lined with fur. Dane examined them a long moment, noting the thick hide, the careful stitches sewing the material together. It gave him an idea.

"Berta, do you have a needle? And maybe some…horse hair?" He tried to ask the question as simply as possible, hoping she would understand. "Also, I need some type of…alcohol."

"Alcohol?" She shook her head, not understanding.

"Yes, like…ale…or…?" What would they have here? He needed something to cleanse the wound and maybe get drunk later.

"Vodka?"

Ding! "That'll work."

She left the tent and returned with a needle, several strands of horse hair and an animal skin flask. The needle was made of bone—thin and sharpened to a fine tip. He glanced at the gaping wound in Skye's shoulder. He could use the bone needle and horse hair and sew up her wound. Most likely she would hate it, but it needed to be done if she were to heal properly.

"Skye?"

She didn't move. He took a deep guzzle from the flask, letting the vodka burn his gut down to his toes. Taking a deep breath, he threaded the needle with the horsehair, his hands shaking. He had never performed such an operation. He knew how, in theory, but he wasn't sure if he could do it. Hell, he couldn't even sew on a button much less sew up a wound. But he had to try, at least.

"Berta, I'll need you to help me. Hold her down in case she fights me because I don't think she'll like this one bit."

Berta moved to sit opposite him, leaning over the unconscious Skye. The lighting in the tent was poor. All he had to see with was the flickering fire. He leaned down close to her, feeling his way along the open wound. It was jagged, under her collarbone and about an inch long. Luckily, it was in the fleshy part of her shoulder, so it should be easy to sew. He poured a splash of vodka in her wound. Her eyes flew open as she sucked in a sharp breath.

"What the devil are you doing?" she said through clenched teeth.

"Cleansing the wound. Hold still."

He knotted the end of the horse hair, took a deep breath and jabbed the bone needle in her skin.

Skye released a high-pitched scream. Berta was there though, and ready, and held her down with her weight.

"What the…ow! That hurts!"

"Hold still, Skye. I'm sewing you up." He sounded calmer than he felt.

"With what? A bloody quilting needle, for Christ's sake?"

"Hold still, will you?"

With shaky fingers, he tugged the first strand taut and then stuck the needle in the other side, completing the first stitch. He repeated this again and again while Skye objected loudly all the while.

"I'm nearly done," he said.

"It feels like you're jabbing me with a hot poker."

"Don't be so dramatic," Dane scoffed.

He tried to sound like it was no big deal, when in fact if their roles had been reversed, he would have been cursing loudly. Her heated objections turned quickly into tears and she sobbed. When Dane made the final stitch, he used his teeth to bite off the excess thread.

"There. All better now." Then he used the vodka once more on her and took a swig for himself.

"No, it's not. It's hurts." Seeing the flask in his hand, she reached for it. "Give me that."

"Skye, it's—"

"I don't give a damn what it is. Give it."

He handed it over. She took a long quaff, scowled as it went down then coughed. "What…?"

"Vodka. I tried to warn you."

Her head hit the makeshift pillow. "Doesn't hurt anymore."

He chuckled as he took back the flask.

As Dane handed the needed back to Berta, he realized she gaped at him in quiet wonder.

"You are a healer," she whispered.

"Hardly," he said.

"You are. I have seen the miracle. You are a healer," she insisted. "Come, we must tell the others."

She took his hand and urged him to his feet. He had no choice but to follow her out of the tent. As he ducked out, he heard Skye mutter, "Healer my ass."

He couldn't agree more.

Chapter 2
Healer

"He is a healer!"

Berta made the announcement as she dragged Dane from the tent by the hand. The men, including the chieftain, sitting by the fire rose. All eyes riveted to him as he hobbled behind the woman.

"I saw with my own eyes. *He is a healer.*"

Odren pinpointed him with his steely gaze. The pipe was still clenched between his yellowed teeth. "Does she speak the truth, stranger?"

"My companion had a wound that needed to be closed," Dane said.

"How did you close it? With magic?" Odren asked, genuinely interested.

"With this!" Berta held aloft the needle. "I saw him do it."

Odren took the needle from her and examined it. "We use this to sew our clothes. You used this to sew her wound?"

Dane nodded. "I did."

Sovold took the needle still stained with Skye's blood. He looked from it to Dane, his eyes narrowing. Dane didn't like that at all.

"It seems you are of some value to us, stranger." Odren removed his pipe, gazed at Dane thoughtfully. "You will accompany us at dawn."

"What happens at dawn?"

"We move southward to meet the neighboring clan, led by the chieftain Nyan," Odren explained. "We will join him there, to strengthen our numbers and hopefully have a meal since game is scarce here."

"She's not ready to move yet," Dane said, thumbing in the direction of Skye's tent. "She's weak still and needs more rest."

"Then you should find a way to move her, healer. Until dawn, I bid you goodnight."

Another dismissal. Dane was starting to feel as though he were in school again.

~ ⧖ ~

Skye slept. Her dreams were vivid ones of her time in Scotland with Malcolm. She could smell his masculine scent, feel his powerful arms around her. Their last kiss was still fresh in her mind and she could feel his lips against hers. She startled awake, her vision clouded with tears.

Or perhaps it was the wood smoke blurring her vision. She lay on her back, staring up at the steepled tent ceiling made of animal bones and skin. She smelled the heady scent of fur near her face, realized then she lay underneath what once had been the pelt of some furry creature. She tried not to gag on the thought of lying under a dead animal.

Under the circumstances, though, it was better than freezing to death. Her gaze flitted across the tiny tent and saw the tattered remains of her once-pretty gown on the ground in a heap. Gingerly, she brushed her fingertips over the wound Dane had sewn for her. He did a decent job, from the feel of things, albeit a painful one. The stitches were small and tight.

A large form entered the tent. At first, she saw only a head of dark hair and assumed it was Dane. But when he lifted his face, she found herself looking into the dark glittering eyes of a scruffy, dirty, unshaven man. It frightened her, sending her heart racing and chills dancing up her spine. And there she was underneath that thick fur with nothing on but her birthday suit.

All she could do was stare back at him, disgusted by his oily, scraggly beard, the dirt on his face and under his fingernails. He knelt at her side, hovering over her with his rancid breath in her face as he licked his dry lips. She lay frozen, unable to move. Even the scream she desperately wanted to release was stuck in her throat.

He reached for her, ran his thick hand through her coppery hair, feeling the strands under his calloused fingers. She shuddered, wondering what he had in mind and fearing what the answer could be. If only Dane was there, this derelict would not even be attempting to manhandle her. Dane wouldn't let him near her. He said he would protect her. So where was he when she needed him?

He leaned down to her and she squeezed her eyes shut, unwilling to see him come so close. She held her breath, waiting for him to do what he wanted and hoped he got out quickly. She could feel his large meaty hands sweeping down her body through the animal pelt and tried to swallow the bile rising in her throat.

"Get away from her."

The deep voice stopped the man and she heard a slight rustle as he stood. Her eyes flew open, relief flooding her as her gaze fell on Dane. Something terrifying flashed in his clear green eyes as he stared down the other man. He stood aside and motioned toward the flap of the tent.

"Get out of here."

The bearded man faced Dane evenly and with fisted hands, but he left the tent without a word. Skye expelled the breath she'd been holding.

"Where were you?"

"Sorry." Dane knelt beside her, tucked the fur around her neck so no skin was exposed. "I was detained."

"I thought he was going to…" She stopped, unable to finish. She could not say the words out loud and forced herself not to think them.

"Who was he?" she asked.

"One of the clansmen. They call him Sovold, I think. I don't like the looks of him. Especially now that he's got an interest in you."

That made her feel better. "I'm glad you showed up when you did."

"Yeah, me too."

"Is this a new fashion statement?" she asked, eyeing his fur-adorned outfit. He'd left wearing his tattered street clothes and returned wearing this.

"It was all the local clothing store had on the racks. The woman, Berta, gave them to me. I'm not sure I trust this chieftain. Name's Odren."

"Why not?"

"I'm pretty good at reading people. I think he's lying to me about how we'll be safe with them. And this other guy…"

"That was scary."

He lay down beside her, laced his fingers and tucked them under his head. "That won't happen again. I promise."

"If it does, maybe you could use those fancy skills on him?" she suggested. "I saw that look in his eye. I know what he meant to do."

He patted her arm over the thick covering. Strangely, it was reassuring.

"Don't worry, Skye. I'll make sure no one harms you. You can count on that."

Was he saying he would protect her? Somehow, a tiny piece of her believed him.

~ ⧗ ~

When dawn arrived, the chieftain came to wake them. He kicked Dane in the ribs. Dane's eyes flew open and he struggled to his feet as quickly as he could, his hands clamping about the chieftain's throat. Eyes wide, Odren coughed and sputtered, trying to catch his breath. Realizing what he'd done, Dane quickly released the chief with a hasty apology.

"We are leaving, healer," Odren croaked, rubbing his neck with his hand, but offering Dane no remonstration for the assault.

Dane scratched his head, forking his fingers through his dark hair as Odren left. Skye yawned, trying to stretch her stiff arms.

"Who was that?" she asked.

"The chieftain." He knelt, placed his hand on her forehead. She was still burning hot. "How do you feel?"

"Hungry. Stiff. Tired," she said. "Where are we going? I don't think I can walk, Dane."

"The chieftain wants to go south and meet another clan. But don't worry, you won't have to."

"Oh? Why's that?"

"I have a plan. Be right back."

Dane hobbled from the tent to find Berta. She seemed to be the only one willing to help him, and only one of three women in the clan. He found her near his tent, wrapping animal skins in a bundle.

"Good morning, Berta," he said with his best winning smile.

She blushed to the roots of her tangled hair. A tiny smile played at the corners of her dirty mouth.

"I need your help with something," Dane said.

"I can only try, healer."

"My companion is still ill and can't walk. I need to make something to carry her on. I'll need something sturdy, like wood or animal bones, and some rope. Do you think you can find these things?"

"I will have the others help me," she said, nodding to the women gawking at him.

"The pieces will need to be long. As tall as a man," he said, and he gestured with his hand toward his chin. "Like to here, like this, see?"

Nodding, Berta lumbered off just as Sovold approached. The boxy man paused in front of Dane, his jaw clenched. Dane immediately put up his defenses. He folded his arms across his chest, blocking the entrance to his tent—and to Skye.

"Let me ask you, healer, is the woman you travel with your mate?" Sovold asked.

Dane contemplated this for a moment, unsure of what his response should be. He went with what he thought would most protect Skye. He didn't like this ugly barbarian asking about Skye, nor did he like he what he had seen the night before. He knew Sovold's intentions were less than honorable.

"She is," Dane said.

"Not for long," Sovold growled and stalked off.

Clearly, the man did not realize with whom he was dealing. Dane decided it was time to arm himself with some kind of weapon. He'd have to keep his eyes open for anything he could use. He would especially have to keep Sovold under his watchful gaze.

Berta returned with the two other wide-eyed females. They carried long, thick pieces of animal bones and several feet of rope. Impressed with their resourcefulness, Dane built a primitive stretcher for Skye. He had the ladies keep the animal bones together while he tied the rope.

"Healer," Odren called. "We go. Come now or you and your lady will be left behind."

"Wait one more moment, please," Dane called back. "Come, Berta."

Picking up the crude stretcher, Dane entered the tent. Skye had passed out again and Dane eased her, grass-bed and all, onto the stretcher.

"Berta, will you help me lift her?"

"How will you travel with her, healer?" she asked.

"Perhaps you would be willing to help?" he suggested.

She sifted from one foot to the other. "I cannot. My mate will not allow that."

"Then one of the others?"

"Larna is without a mate. She will help you carry your lady."

"Very well, then."

~ ⧖ ~

They walked until nightfall. The temperatures dropped. The wind was colder. Snow began to fall, and Skye shivered uncontrollably under the thick fur. Dane worried about her. Her teeth chattered, and she still burned with fever.

"Dane," Skye whispered. "It's so cold."

"I know. I'm sorry." He patted her forehead, trying to reassure her. "Hopefully we'll be at the other village tomorrow. Odren said they were bigger and would accept this clan into theirs."

She shuddered, trying to ward off the chill. She licked her dry lips.

"I'll find you some fresh water." He rose, glancing around.

"No," she croaked. "Don't leave me."

"Are you sure?"

She managed a nod. He sat on the ground beside her. Odren walked over and peered down at Skye, his deep brown eyes examining her with interest.

"She will live?" he asked.

Dane didn't like his interest in her. "She's quite ill. She needs medicine."

"What is…medicine?" Odren asked with a frown, pronouncing the unfamiliar word slowly, carefully.

"It can help heal her," Dane said. "A fever has taken hold of her. It would help make her better."

"You have none?" Odren crossed his thick arms over his chest. When Dane shook his head, his bushy eyebrow raised, and he looked thoughtful. Then he said, "Perhaps Nyan's shaman can help you. I will speak to him when we arrive."

Odren returned to his place by the fire. He and Sovold exchanged a few words as they glanced their way.

"What's he up to?" she whispered.

"I don't know," Dane agreed. "I don't like this sudden interest in you."

As he tucked the fur around her neck trying to keep the cold off her skin, he hoped her fever would break soon. Motion caught his eye. He glanced up to see Sovold's big form lumbering toward them. He carried a small cup in his meaty hand and wore an unnerving grin. Dane rose to his full height, his fists clenched as he locked eyes with the man.

"You are parched. Drink this." He handed Dane the cup, its contents steaming.

"No, thanks." He eyed the drink skeptically. "I'd rather not."

"A peace offering," Sovold said. "Take it as acceptance or risk insulting the chieftain."

"What happens if I insult him?"

"You will be banished here. Left to survive alone without the clan." His gaze flickered to Skye then back to Dane.

Oh, he got the significance of that. Sovold wanted him out of the way so he could get to her. Not on his watch. He took the cup. Sovold grinned broadly, a strange twinkle in his eyes. He said nothing more as he walked away, leaving Dane holding the cup.

Chapter 3
Changing of the Guard

"You aren't going to drink that, are you?" Skye eyed the wooden cup in his hand.

Dane sniffed it, wrinkled his nose. Glancing up, he saw Sovold watched him with a baleful stare. Even for a man as cunning as Dane, it sent a prickle of fear through him. He turned his back to Sovold, something he knew was probably a mistake.

"He's watching," Dane said. "He's waiting for me to drink it, I think."

Before she could answer, the crunch of snow nearby stopped her. Larna, the young woman who had helped to carry Skye, appeared and squatted down across from Dane. She twirled her tangled hair around a forefinger and reached for the wooden cup, slipping it from Dane's grasp.

"Do not drink, healer." Her voice was low and gruff. "It is poison." She poured the liquid out on the frozen ground.

Unable to help himself, Dane glanced over his shoulder. Berta had distracted Sovold by sitting in his lap, her legs wrapped around his hips.

"I saw the chieftain give him the poison," Larna explained. "I told Berta. She wished to help you, healer, as did I."

"You seem to have some fans," Skye said dryly, one eyebrow raised.

"Skye, this is Larna. She helped me carry you today."

"I see." Skye gave her a half smile. "I'll be walking tomorrow."

"Are you sure?" Dane placed his hand on her forehead. "You still have a fever."

"My joints are stiff, Dane," she said. "I need the movement. There's only one problem."

"What's that?"

"I have nothing to wear."

~ ⧖ ~

Thanks to Larna, Skye was outfitted in the same animal skins and furs as everyone else. They resumed their trek through the frozen tundra the next morning. Her shoulder ached, leaving her arm stiff. She still felt like she had been hit by a truck, but she couldn't stand the thought of that uncomfortable stretcher anymore. She balked when she found out it was made from animal bones.

"Don't complain," Dane had said. "It was that or nothing."

"I would have preferred nothing."

She found, though, she had a difficult time walking. Her legs ached. Her joints were stiff from the cold. Dane stayed with her, bringing up the rear of the clan and letting her hold onto him whenever she needed it. He still hobbled with his broken leg. She couldn't fathom how he managed to carry her stretcher all that way with his injury. She was grateful for him.

"Dane, you do still have the time bender, right?" she asked.

"Yes, I've still got it." His voice was thick and raspy in her ear. She could hear his labored breathing. "It's in my pocket."

"Do you think it's reset itself by now?"

"Ready to leave, are you?"

He flashed a dazzling grin, yet she could tell it was offered through pain. Beads of perspiration dotted his forehead. She tightened her arm around his waist as they continued to trudge through the snow. The barren brown landscape had changed once again the further south they moved. Snow covered the ground, though it was only a few inches deep.

"Are you all right? Perhaps you should be leaning on *me*," she suggested. Her brow creased with worry.

"Fine," he puffed, his breath crystallizing on the air. "Just a bit tired."

"How's the ankle?"

"Achy. I doubt it will ever be the same."

She suddenly had a pang of sorrow and regret shoot through her. Their predicament was because of her. His sprained ankle was because of her, as was her wounded shoulder. She wondered about Thomas and if he was all right. Had he managed to escape from whoever shot up the old tech building? And what of Conner and the hit man?

"Dane, I'm so sorry," she said then and frowned. It was all she could think to say.

"Sorry for what? It's not your fault I twisted by ankle."

"I feel responsible. You're here because of me, aren't you?"

Before he could answer, riders on horseback appeared in the distance, thundering over the snow-covered ground. He paused to stare at the small cluster headed their way. The rest of Odren's clan halted, huddled together while Skye and Dane remained a distance behind them.

"Odd," he muttered.

"What is?" She followed his gaze, watched the riders. There did seem to be something out of place with them.

"Look at them," he said. "I mean, really *look* at them."

She peered at the small group riding closer, her eyes squinting against the morning glare. They seemed a cluster, but as they neared, she counted five horsemen. Every rider had a saddle on their horse. They wore leather boots and what looked like cotton uniforms underneath their fur. The man, who seemed to be the leader as he rode in front of the other four, had a sword at his side, the morning sun glinting off the steel blade.

"I don't get it," Skye said.

"Me, either," Dane said. "Look around us. These people live like cavemen or something—Cro-Magnon or Neanderthal. How is it they're wearing animal skins and fur and those riders are wearing leather and cotton? And he has a weapon. A steel blade not a crude spear."

"Maybe we're not in the past after all."

"That's what scares me." Dane's eyes riveted to the riders. "If not, then where are we? The future?"

"I have no idea." She shook her head and clutched his waist tighter against her.

The leader unsheathed his sword. Chieftain Odren and his small clan stood in the snow, watching their approach.

"What do we do?"

He glanced around, saw an outcropping to their left. The wind picked up as it started to snow. "Come on. We can get behind there."

The snow started falling heavily enough to cover their tracks almost as soon as they made them, concealing their dash to the hiding place. Dane lowered himself to the ground with a grunt, unable to kneel and see what was happening.

"Keep your eye on the riders," he said. "I want to know what's happening."

Skye stooped in the snow next to him, peering over the edge of the rock. Her hair billowed in the wind around her face and she fought to keep it out of her vision. Heat radiated from her cheeks. She knew it was the fever. Despite that, she shivered.

"The one with the sword is galloping toward the group," she said. "No one is moving. Why do they stand there?"

"Maybe they know him?" Dane suggested.

"Nyan?"

She heard Odren's confusion on the wind.

The man on horseback, Nyan, stopped. They had words she couldn't hear. It was nothing more than muffled sound on the wind. Then Nyan charged forward and sliced his sword through the air. It connected with the chieftain's throat. Blood spurted and Odren crumbled to the snow. She gasped, covering her mouth to stifle a scream and ducked to the snow next to Dane.

"What happened? You're white as the snow."

"The...the rider..." she stammered. "He killed the chieftain." She hiccupped the words as her throat constricted. She gripped Dane's animal fur covering in her fists. "We have to get out of here."

"Those who would follow Odren," boomed a strange voice. "Will belong to my tribe from henceforth!"

"Get up and see who's talking." Dane nudged her with his elbow.

She flashed him her best heated look before she raised herself onto her knees and peered over the edge of the outcropping again. Odren lay in the blood-stained snow facedown.

"It's the leader, the one with the sword who killed Odren."

"There is a new order here," the rider called out. "Any of you who oppose will meet the same fate as Odren. Vigor, make sure they are bound. I want no escapees before we reach camp."

"One of his men is dismounting," Skye whispered to Dane. "He has a bunch of rope. He's tying their wrists together, and then binding...oh, shit!" She inhaled sharply and then ducked down. "Sovold pointed me out. They saw me."

"Christ," he muttered. "We can't escape. Not with both of us injured."

Skye slipped her hand into his, grasping his fingers with a tight squeeze. "Maybe we should try the time bender now."

"You said we could only use it once every—"

"I know what I said, but maybe I'm wrong," she snapped. They could hear the drumming of the horse's hooves pounding the ground. "Just try it. Push the damn button."

He shifted his weight and reached beneath his fur-lined coat. He pulled out the time bender and held it between them. Skye squeezed his hand. She hoped it would work as his thumb depressed the button.

Nothing happened. They were stuck there.

"Get up." The raw voice came from the man named Vigor as he leaned over the outcropping to look at them. Two other soldiers came quickly into view.

"Tie them up," Vigor ordered.

"Please don't do that," Skye said. "He's injured. He won't be able to walk if you bind us together."

"That is not my concern," Vigor spat.

"Please, I beg you," Skye said.

Vigor's eyes narrowed as he looked at her. She wanted to squirm under his steel gaze but forced herself to remain still. He reached for a lock of her hair and rubbed it between thumb and forefinger.

"Hair like the flames…"

She clenched her fists to keep from slapping his hand away. Beside her, Dane stiffened. Even he knew reacting would get him hurt or, worse, killed.

"Your companion's comfort is of no importance to me. However, I will grant your request. I will not bind you together," Vigor said.

"Thank you," Skye said, relieved.

"Comrade, bring the girl to me and bind the man's wrists," Vigor said to his guard.

"But you said—" she began.

"I would not bind you together," he interrupted. "Come quietly, girl, or face the consequences even your looks cannot save you from. And I assure you, you do not want to face them."

She was shoved roughly away from Dane, their linked hands ripped apart.

"Leave her alone." Dane stepped forward, but the henchman shoved him back.

"She is no longer your concern," Vigor said. "She is mine."

With the help of one of the men, she was lifted into the saddle in front of Vigor. She turned, watching as Dane's wrists were bound together and then his fur was stripped away from his shoulders. Vigor fingered her copper locks again, inhaled the scent of her hair.

"If you do that, he'll freeze," she said, her teeth clenched. It took all her self-control to allow him to continue to touch her. "At least allow him to have a fighting chance by staying warm."

Vigor wrapped his arms around her, clasping the reins in front of her, pulling her to him. She could feel his hardened body against hers.

"Do you have some sort of allegiance to this man, my dear? Hmm?" Then to the others, "Give him the fur." As they threw it back to Dane, Vigor whispered in her ear again, his hot breath tickling her skin. "But know this—it is the last request I will grant you."

As he galloped away, Skye could not stop looking at Dane as he hobbled along in the snow. Vigor reined in the horse when they neared the circle of men. The horse snorted, its breath exhaling in a white fog. Skye forced herself not to shiver against the hulking man behind her.

"Chieftain Nyan, I found more clansmen," Vigor stated. "They were hiding behind the outcropping."

The leader gazed at her with dark eyes. "Your prize, Vigor? She's quite a beauty."

"I should like to keep her for myself." Vigor nuzzled her neck. She jerked her head away.

Fear prickled at the back of her throat and she swallowed hard. She would have to find a way out of this and soon, or who knows what would become of them.

"We can discuss it later." Nyan mounted his horse. "Let's get moving. Night will fall soon, and we need to be indoors. Make sure the prisoners keep up."

"As you wish, chieftain." Vigor gave a respectful bow of the head.

Skye chewed her lower lip, trying to come up with an escape plan. Being separated from Dane was not good. She knew that for sure. She would have to find a way to get back to him. He had the time bender and they had to get home somehow. It hadn't worked when they'd tried it only moments earlier, but it was still too soon, according to the window Thomas Hardy had warned her about. The seventy-two-hour waiting period was nearly over.

Turning westward, they crested a ridge as the sun kissed the horizon. It sent a shimmering glow across the crisp white snow. Skye was momentarily blinded by the brightness. She shielded her eyes as they turned southwest and headed straight for—

All thought froze in her mind as she stared ahead, trying to comprehend yet another new development. What she saw sent a flurry of questions through her mind. How could it be?

They headed straight for a metal building. It looked like the remains of an abandoned military outpost. The building was huge, with big double doors. It confirmed her thought they had landed in the future.

As they neared the building, she saw faded markings in white near the double doors. Her heart throbbed in her chest. While she could not read them, she did recognize the symbols. The words were written in Russian.

With the shock still roiling through her, she glanced back at Dane. He, too, was staring at the building, eyes wide with surprise. He caught her glance, knit his brows, and shook his head.

Wherever they were, she thought, it was likely they were with the enemy.

Chapter 4
Prisoner of Fate

The heavy double doors slid open, creaking and grinding. Vigor's breath was heavy in Skye's ear and then she felt his cold nose nudge against her. It sent a sick feeling of fear and disgust through her. She sat rock-still in the saddle, refusing to move one inch. She tried not to imagine the horrible things he probably wanted to do to her.

They entered the building which looked more like a large hangar used not for airplanes, but animals. She could hear the buzz of overhead fluorescent lights. Each side was lined with stalls, each containing horses and cows. She thought she heard pigs squealing and chickens clucking from nearby, as well. There were several people mucking the stalls. They spoke to each other in a language that sounded like Russian.

Nyan pulled his horse to a stop and dismounted, stripping off leather gloves. "Bring her to me." He spoke English, so the captives would understand him.

Vigor dismounted, and then grasped Skye by the waist. He swung her down from the horse with ease, as if she weighed nothing. She had to admit, his strength was impressive. Terrifying, but impressive. Vigor gave her a shove toward the leader.

"Lovely." Nyan smiled as he brushed the back of his hand across her cheek.

His teeth weren't yellow stumps like those of the people in Odren's clan. His eyes were black as coal, his hair the same color, long and wavy. He had a shadow of beard covering his chin and throat. His flawless complexion was a warm cappuccino color, dark and creamy all at once. He had a strong square jaw and misshapen nose, as though it had been broken numerous times.

"I have not seen hair this color." His voice was low and throaty. He touched Skye's auburn locks, curling a tendril around his thick forefinger. She couldn't help but notice how large his hands were. Her heart pattered a quick, anxious cadence in her chest.

"She is mine." Vigor placed a hand on her shoulder, as if to claim her. She winced from the pain of her wound.

"Do you think that wise, Vigor?" Nyan turned his black gaze on his man. "After all, you are not a chieftain. Your men will fight for her if they know she belongs to you. We both know how volatile they are."

"Perhaps."

Skye could hear the disdain in Vigor's stilted tone. A thin smiled crossed Nyan's face as he turned his gaze back to her. "She is fitting for a chieftain. No one would dare challenge me for her." He extended his hand. "Come with me, my dear."

She hesitated, staring at his empty palm. She held her breath, choosing her words wisely. She had to make certain Dane would be all right. "What of the others?" she asked.

"Some will be sent to work for the clan like the others." He waved toward the men mucking stalls. "Others will be taken to a holding cell until their fate is determined."

"Will they be unharmed?"

Nyan's brows drew together in annoyance. "IT is not for you to worry over, my dear. The guards have their own way with the prisoners."

Skye glanced behind her, saw them being taken away. Dane still hobbled on his injured ankle, his wrists bound. She folded her arms.

"I want your word they will not be harmed." She never took her eyes off Dane.

An exasperated sigh escaped Nyan before he replied. "Very well. Vigor, see to it personally the prisoners are treated well—by order of the chieftain."

"Yes, my liege." Vigor bowed before turning on his heel and following the prisoners. Skye was aware of the hardened glare he gave her as he left.

"Now…" Nyan held his hand out to her once again. "Will you come?"

She had no other choice. She slipped her hand into his and followed him from the large converted hangar. He led her into a drafty, narrow corridor with flickering lights. They turned a corner, leaving her to feel as though she was in a maze of hallways. The further into the building they went, the warmer it seemed to get. Nyan pulled off the fur covering his spotless uniform.

"You will want to remove your outer coverings," he said. "This part of the building is quite warm."

Tentatively, she removed her fur. She was surprised by the warmth flowing through the small area. He paused outside a door, pressed a button on a panel. The door whooshed open and he motioned her inside.

The room was sparse and drab. Everything seemed to be the same color, a dull, steely gray. A metal desk strewn with papers stood in one corner. Behind it, she saw a floor-to-ceiling metal bookcase littered with books and trinkets, a crystal decanter filled with an amber liquid. A computer was on one side of the desk, giving a sense of familiarity, as though something was normal. On the other side of the room was a large unmade bed with a metal frame.

"Sit." He motioned to the bed.

"What are you going to do with me?" She perched on the side of the mattress.

"You are wounded, are you not?" he asked. She gave a nod. "I will see to it my personal healer attends you.

Something to drink?" He poured a glass of the light-brown liquid and extended it to her.

"No, thanks." She shivered and cradled the fur to her chest.

Nyan downed the drink, then set aside the glass on the desk. He walked toward her, his boots scuffling the floor. He paused, staring at her with a hardened gaze she didn't like one bit. "Now, my dear, tell me why you are here and who you are working for."

"Wh-what do you mean?" she stammered.

"You and your male companion were hiding behind an outcropping. I want to know why," he demanded.

He folded his thick arms across his chest. She could see the ripples of muscles underneath the material of his uniform.

"I don't work for anyone." She stared up at him with wide eyes.

"Did Yuris send you? Are you his spy?" His hand wrapped around her bicep as he dragged her to her feet. "Tell me the truth and no games, girl."

"I *am* telling you the truth." Fear bubbled inside her, yet she was determined not to show it. "My companion and I don't work for anyone. I swear it. We lost everything and Odren and his people took us in after we..."

She clamped her mouth shut.

"After you what?"

Her throat turned dry. She couldn't tell him the truth. "After we made it to his camp."

He shoved her to the bed, turned on his heel and stomped away. Skye sank into the mattress, still clutching the fur to her. She tried to stop shivering but couldn't. Her teeth wanted to chatter, but she forced her mouth to remain closed. She was terrified of this man. She saw the anger and hatred in his cold black stare.

"I have no idea who Yuris is," she added, her voice timid in the room.

Nyan looked at her over his shoulder. "Where do you come from, then?"

She hesitated, unsure how to answer. She couldn't tell him anything about the time bender or how they came to be here in this frozen tundra. "We came from a faraway land."

Nyan reached for the decanter again, poured another glass and then downed it in one gulp. She watched as his fingers circled the rim of the glass and he spoke calmly.

"You appear to be telling the truth. Therefore, I will accept your word and trust you. But know this, girl." He fixed her with his hardened black stare, sending shivers through her. "If you have lied to me, if you or your companion betrays my trust, I will kill you both."

Skye nodded as she swallowed the lump of fear in her throat. "I understand," she whispered.

"I will send my healer," he said then, heading for the door.

He left her alone, sitting on the edge of the bed, clutching her fur. She vehemently wished Dane was with her. At least she knew she could trust him.

~ ⧗ ~

Her dreams were erratic. From images of her father being shot to Malcolm Wallace in Scotland to the horror of what happened in the snow with the old chieftain. As though she were reliving all the horrible things once again in her nightmares.

She startled awake, sitting upright in the bed trying to get her hammering heart under control. Glancing around, she remembered everything that had happened and where she was.

"Rest, little one."

Her head snapped in the direction of the strange voice. An old woman sat near the bed, her gnarled hands curled in her lap. Her face was a roadmap of winkles, her skin color the same dusky hue as Nyan's. Her long dark hair was streaked with silver and pulled back at the nape of her neck. She gave Skye a crumpled smile and rose. Pale blue eyes peered out of an aged faced.

She was short, hunched over. The old woman shuffled to her bedside, reached for her. Skye flinched, jerking away from her.

"Calm, little one. I will not harm you."

She reached for Skye's shoulder where she had been wounded, gently peeling away a fresh and unfamiliar bandage. Skye couldn't remember when or how it had come to be there. In fact, all she could recall after Nyan had left was lying down on the bed and drifting into a restless sleep. She had no idea how long she had been out. Now she glanced down at her shoulder, the wound Dane had sewn only days before. There was nothing more than a silvery scar.

"How did you…?" Skye began, but her voice trailed away. She gingerly touched the scar with her fingertips. "I don't understand."

"It is not meant for you to, little one." Another crumpled smile. "I am Ilsa."

"Are you the healer Nyan spoke of?" Skye asked.

"Healer?" Ilsa chuckled and shuffled back to her chair by the bedside. "I am many things. Today I am the healer."

Confused, Skye wrinkled her brow. "You healed me, then."

"You had a fever with your wound. It was infected. I thought you might die."

"Thank you for your help."

"It was nothing. IT gave me use." She waved it away. "Nyan tells many people many things, but he did not tell you about me? Other than I was the healer."

"No."

"I am Nyan's *maman*. His mother." She winked.

"Oh," Skye gasped. "It's a pleasure to make your acquaintance."

"Tell me, little one, what was it you did to make my son so angry."

"I did nothing." Skye ran a hand through her tangled hair. "He doesn't understand who I am."

"And who are you?"

Skye peered at her, biting her lower lip. "No one of importance."

She chuckled. "I do not believe such a thing. Your hair is the color of flame. Your skin nearly white as the snow. And your eyes…well, no one has seen eyes that color before."

Skye clutched the bed covers to her chest, acutely aware of her looks. They had gotten her free drinks at bars and sometimes a hot date, but something told her she stuck out like a sore thumb here.

"My son knows you are not from this place. As do I. Where are you from, little one?"

She swallowed hard. "Far away."

She smiled again. "That I do believe. You should tell him."

"How long have I been here?" Skye changed the subject, not wishing to discuss where she was really from.

"You slept for many days."

"Days?" Skye blinked, alarmed as she thought of Dane in the holding cell. She hoped he was all right. Was he still there? Would he use the time bender and leave her behind? As soon as the thought struck her, she dismissed it. He promised to protect her and so far, he'd made good on that promise.

"I've got to get out of here." She flung back the bedding and got to her feet.

"Hold, little one." Ilsa rose and put a hand on her shoulder to stop her. "It would not be wise to leave. You may be considered an escapee."

An escapee? Skye frowned. "Am I a prisoner here, then?"

Before Ilsa could reply, the door slid open and Nyan entered. He carried a large rectangular box and stopped short when he saw the two of them. He spoke rapidly in his native tongue. His tone was less than friendly. His mother snapped back.

After a few moments of a heated debate, Nyan shook his head. "Leave us," he said now in English to Ilsa.

She turned to Skye with a small grin. "My son seems to think you're a spy. But I know better, don't I?" She patted her arm and then rose. "You should tell him, little one."

Tell him she was a time traveler? No way.

"*Maman*," Nyan said through gritted teeth.

"As you wish, my son."

The old woman gave a nod and did as he ordered, scuffling from the room. The door sealed quietly behind her and Skye faced Nyan alone once more. He extended the box to her.

"Take it," he ordered.

She pushed aside the lid and found a very revealing outfit inside. She shuddered as she picked it up to examine more closely. The dress had a plunging top with cap sleeves and a very short skirt. Accompanying the outfit were knee-high boots lined with wool.

Terrific. She was going to look like a prehistoric hooker.

She fingered the supple material. It felt like suede. Nothing good would come from her wearing it. She had to get out of there and soon.

"You will put that on," Nyan told her.

"Now?" Skye asked.

"I will wait outside if you wish."

"I wish." Yeah, like she was going to strip down in front of him. *Pervert.*

"Do not tarry."

She watched him leave, wishing for this strange nightmare to be over.

~ ⧖ ~

"What are you planning to do with her?" Ilsa demanded in their native tongue when her son appeared in the corridor.

Her rigid frame stood as tall as her petite stature would allow, her hands clasped in front of her tiny frame. She may have been ancient, but she was still his mother and she could demand things from him. She knew something was to come of the strange girl's arrival with the savages.

"That is not your concern." Nyan's stride never broke as he headed down the hallway.

"I am your *maman.*" She grabbed his arm and yanked him to a stop. "I asked you about your intentions."

Nyan paused, his black glare fixed on his mother's face. She could see his mind working and knew he was up to something. She never knew her son to be distracted by even the most comely of women. This turn of events, his inexplicable interest in the girl surprised and worried Ilsa.

"I have made a deal with one of the savages," he said at last. "I will give her to him. She will become his wife. It will be a *troskian* ceremony."

Ilsa's eyes widened. She released her grip on her son's arm, the blood draining from her face. The *troskian* wedding ceremony was ancient and cruel. And irreversible. "You cannot do that to her," she whispered, her voice faint.

"It is the only way to ensure peace among the tribes," Nyan said. "Is that not what you want? What you have begged me to pursue all these long years? It is what my father wanted."

"Yes, my son, but not like this," Ilsa said. "Not by forcing that poor girl to—"

"The one who proclaims to be the new leader—this Sovold—has assured me if I turn her over to him, he and his people will join us without a fight." Nyan ran his hand down his face and expelled a breath. "What would you have of me, *maman?* I have been asked to trade one life for countless. One girl I do not know in exchange for the lives of my soldiers and friends, my tribemates and fellows. War is coming. You know as well as I. I need all the men I can get, even the savages. Killing their leader ensured they would join but they were more resistant than I anticipated. Do you not see? I have no other choice."

Ilsa was quiet for a long moment. "There are always other choices."

"The girl fulfills the prophecy. I gave my word. I do not intend to break it."

"I hope you have made the right choice, then, my son."

"As do I, *maman.* As do I." He sighed then, glancing at Skye's door before heading down the corridor.

Ilsa watched him go, knew he was tormented by the decision. Perhaps it was time she took matters into her own hands.

Chapter 5
Marriage Made in Hell

Skye stared at the soft suede for a long moment. She ran her hand over it and marveled at the smoothness. She glanced around the room, searching for a mirror. She found one desperately in need of cleaning in what she supposed was the bathroom. At least, it looked like a bathroom. There was a toilet and a crude shower.

Oh, what she wouldn't give for a shower. She reached for the faucet, turned on the water. It sputtered before streaming to life. She grinned from ear to ear, testing the water with her fingertips. She stripped and stepped under the scalding shower. She only stayed in a few luxurious, wonderful moments, just enough to rinse off the dirt. She didn't want to linger too long, fearing Nyan would come back and see her.

She toweled off quickly. She was sliding the suede dress over her head when she heard the door to the chamber open. She froze, staring at her foggy reflection. Her hair was wild about her face, and there were dark circles under her eyes. She listened to booted footsteps coming closer and held her breath.

Nyan's image appeared in the mirror behind her. He paused, dark eyes meeting hers. She waited for him to speak. When he never did, she whirled around, faced him, her hands on her hips.

"Well?" she demanded.

His gaze raked over her, leaving her feeling exposed and self-conscious. Why did men from her own time never look at her like that? Instead she had to travel backwards and forwards in time in order to be ogled like a piece of meat.

"You will be married," Nyan said then.

Skye shook her head, startled. "*What?*"

"Everything is arranged," he said. "It is the only way to achieve peace."

Here we go again. Why did men think a marriage would obtain peace and solve everything?

"Sometimes, you're all are so dimwitted." She puffed out an annoyed breath.

"Excuse me?" Nyan blinked in surprise.

"Nothing," she muttered, shaking her head again. "Who am I supposed to marry?"

"Sovold," he replied matter-of-factly.

Her breath caught in her throat. She wasn't exactly sure she heard him right. "Who did you say?" she said, her voice a faint whisper.

"Sovold leads the savages now. He has agreed to a peace treaty with us in exchange for you."

"And you *agreed?*"

"It is the only way."

"No, it's not!" She grabbed his shirtfront, yanking him toward her. "I beg you, Nyan. Don't give me to him. Please don't."

"I cannot argue with you," he snapped, shoving her away. "It is done. By dawn, you will be his and I will have my signed treaty and at least peace between the clans."

He started to walk away, but she couldn't let him go so easily.

"I'm surprised at you, Nyan." Her voice was harsh and cold. He turned, gave her a questioning look. "You bend so easily to those you call 'savages.' And for what? The price of a woman? I saw you kill Odren. I know you are powerful." She took a tentative step toward him. "Sometimes peace comes with the price of war."

"You know not of what you speak. You know nothing of this place or our battles."

"That's true," she agreed. "Do you honestly think it won't cause any more bloodshed? This marriage?"

"There's been enough," Nyan said. "And I will not allow my people to be slain any more. Sleep well, pretty one. In the morning, the ceremony will commence."

She watched her last hope leave. The door slid shut and locked with a quiet finality. She moved to the bed, sank into the mattress once again. She had hoped to convince him to let her go. Perhaps if she could have, she could reach Dane to find out if he was still alive. She had no idea what had become of the other prisoners.

Apparently, though, Sovold had somehow gained Nyan's trust. It surprised her. She had thought Sovold wasn't that smart. How was it he had gained so much access to Nyan in these last few days? And why would any war between Nyan's more technologically endowed people and the primitive savages of Sovold's ranks be at war for any length of time to begin with? Nyan and his people were far more advanced than those simpletons. They should have been able to easily rid themselves of such enemies.

She was confused. She had seen Nyan kill the chieftain, Odren, on the tundra and the others had cowered before him. Clearly, he was powerful, a born leader. How could Sovold have gotten to him and convinced him to marry her off?

She knew Sovold wanted Dane out of the way to get to her. The realization slammed into her hard, turning her stomach. She shuddered, hugging her elbows.

She hoped Dane was all right.

~ ⧖ ~

Dane's wrists were shackled to the wall in iron manacles. His arms had long ago gone numb. He couldn't feel his fingers anymore either. His sprained ankle, though somewhat healed, still throbbed. It seemed years ago since that had happened.

His head drooped forward, his vision blurry, though from sweat or blood, he really didn't know any more. From the moment he had been imprisoned, the guards used him as a punching bag. If he could get out of those manacles, he could…what? Fight back?

He heaved a sigh, wondering what had become of Skye. He worried about her with that chieftain fellow, Nyan. Even if he could get to the time bender, he'd never leave Skye behind.

He had to find some way to get out of this cell. But even if he could, he wasn't sure how far he would get. He was half-dead from starvation. The guards would only allow him a trickle of water. Just enough to keep him alive. Just before they would beat him again.

A drop of blood oozed into his swollen left eye. He blinked, trying to make it go away. It seemed to blur his vision even more. He could hear muffled voices and closed his eyes. He could stand torture. He was no weakling. But there was only so much a man could take before breaking.

Footsteps paused outside his cell, and then he heard the clank of the key in the lock. The heavy metal door creaked open and then silence. Dane stared at a pair of booted feet and knew it was Sovold before him.

"Now, healer, it is time to meet your maker."

The guards unlocked his wrists, letting his arms fall limply to his side. He crumpled to the cold metal floor, his fingers tingling painfully as the blood rushed back to the tips. The guards picked him up under his arms and dragged him out of the cell, leading him down a shadowy corridor.

"Put him there," Sovold demanded.

The men lifted Dane and placed him on a metal table. He shivered, staring into a bright light overhead. Sovold leaned over, directly into Dane's line of sight, and gave a wicked smile.

"Look at you now, healer. You are at my mercy. Who will save you?"

He moved away momentarily, snapping at the guards. "Strap him down. Make sure he cannot get free." Then he appeared once again in Dane's sight. "Before you die, I thought you should know your female companion and I are to be married."

Dane struggled to sit up, straining to reach Sovold's neck but the guards held him down. Sovold gave a hearty chuckle.

"Leave…her…alone," Dane croaked.

"Or what? There is nothing you can do. She is mine at last and I have secured my position with Nyan." He disappeared out of Dane's view, but Dane could hear him pacing nearby. "For many moons, I have worked to make it so. When you and the flame-haired girl arrived, it was the first sign. When Nyan killed Odren, it was the second sign. It was time for me to set my plan into action." His feet scuffed the floor as he came to a halt. "Odren was a fool for cowering against Nyan and his people." He leaned over, looking at Dane once again. "You make a worthy adversary. I hate to kill you."

"You make a worthy adversary. I hate to die," Dane said.

Sovold scowled at his pithy reply and looked to his men. "Kill him now."

Dane turned his head, saw a beefy man headed toward him with a syringe in his hand. There was nothing he could do but accept whatever poison it was. He would die, leaving Skye alone here, helpless against this rotten son of a bitch and his wretched lot. He only hoped she could find the time bender and get back home before something happened to her.

The man stood next to him now and shoved up his sleeve. The tip of the needle pressed against Dane's flesh, digging into the bend of his elbow. He closed his eyes, sucking in a hissing breath between his teeth as he felt it sink into his arm. A loud explosion rocked the room, shuddering the table, and the man with the syringe screamed. Dane opened his eyes but couldn't see what was happening. The room filled with a choking cloud of smoke. He could hear the shouts of the men off to his right, frightened, panicked cries.

"Move away."

The voice that spoke above the din was aged and female.

"He is mine to kill!" Dane heard Sovold cry out in choked protest.

"I'm afraid you've worn out your welcome, Sovold. Now step away from him before I have to make you."

"You are making a grave mistake, Ilsa," Sovold said. "I shall tell Nyan."

"Tell him, then," Ilsa said. "I have more power over him than you'll ever know."

"This is far from over. Come, men. We have a wedding to attend."

Dane strained his ears, heard receding footsteps running from the room. The woman then appeared next to him, leaning over the table and into his view. She had a kind but wrinkled face. Her dark eyes were bright and sharp. Her long black hair was sprinkled with graying stands that fell over her shoulders. She patted his shoulder with a gnarled hand.

"Rest easy now, son. You are safe." Her hands worked quickly, surprising Dane. She removed the needle still stuck in his arm, then removed his bindings. She helped him to a sitting position. He gripped the edge of the metal table to steady himself.

For such a small woman in stature, she exuded great strength and power. Dane could sense it from her touch and knew she was someone who meant business.

"Who are you?"

"I have come to release you," she said. "Tell me, is the woman offered to Sovold your traveling companion?"

"Yes." A tingling sensation of fear went through him.

"You must go to her at once. Get her out of here."

"How?" Dane asked. "I'm too weak to walk and my ankle is still swollen."

"Ah, but you will soon be healed." She smiled, her face crinkling. "I have come to mend you, son."

"Why?" Dane gave her a cautious look.

"Your companion is being offered to Sovold in a *troskian* ceremony. It is a marriage rite. She will be forced to drink a potion, binding her to him forever. She will be subdued so he may do with her as he wishes. She will be his slave."

A sick feeling crept through him. First, Robert Bruce, now this. Skye didn't deserve to be treated as nothing more than property.

"What kind of world is this?"

Ilsa unwrapped his soiled banding still binding his ankle.

"You must trust me. Do you?" she asked.

Should he trust her? He didn't know her, though she did manage to keep Sovold from killing her. Finally, he nodded.

She reached into a small bag at her side and pulled out a vial. She uncorked it and sprinkled something that looked like sand in the palm of her hand. She placed the vial back in her bag and then rubbed her hands together vigorously. A white cloud emerged from her palms and settled over him. She placed her hands on his knee then slid them down to his swollen ankle. He felt a mild burning sensation on his skin, then it went deeper, as though touching his muscles.

"It will pass," she said. "Remain calm and all will be well."

She made another pass from knee to ankle and suddenly the throbbing disappeared. The swelling was gone. Ilsa reached back into her bag and removed another tiny vial. This one was full of a ruby liquid. She opened it and handed it to him.

"Drink," she ordered.

"What is it?" He wrinkled his nose, refusing to take it.

"You need strength. This will give it to you. Take it and drink." She pushed it toward him.

Dane took it, held it tentatively and hesitated. He stared at the ruby liquid, sniffed it. It smelled heady and faintly spicy, like a good red wine.

"There is not much time if you wish to save her," Ilsa said.

"Here goes nothing." He downed the liquid in one gulp and handed back the vial. He smacked his lips, savoring the after-flavors. Cabernet sauvignon. Definitely.

"Now, you must arm yourself." She reached one last time in her bag and produced a small dagger. "It will be less conspicuous than a broadsword."

"Right." He might have hoped for an assault rifle, or at least a semi-automatic pistol with a thirteen-round clip, but beggars couldn't be choosers, and a blade was better than nothing. Dane took the knife, sheathing it in his belt. "Thank you."

The old woman smiled. "Good luck, son. May the gods favor you."

Chapter 6
Always a Bride

The morning came far quicker than she wanted. She hadn't slept at all. At least Nyan had a servant bring her breakfast, not that she could eat much. Her stomach was in knots.

Where was Dane? How was she going to get out of this mess?

Skye paced the confines of the small room, biting her thumbnail. She wished she could come up with a plan to get out of this mess. She wished she could get to Dane, or at least find out if he was still alive and still in the holding cell.

She had to believe he was still alive and would find some way to get to her, though how she didn't know. She was locked inside this room with no way out. She sat on the edge of the bed, frowning when the door whooshed open. Her heart leaped behind her ribcage when she saw Nyan enter, followed by several guards.

"Come," he said. "It is time."

She hesitated, not moving from the bed, and he took a large step toward her, grabbing her by the arm. "Do not force me to use…unpleasant methods, girl."

A terrifying glare matched his tone of warning. He meant business. Reluctantly, Skye followed him out of his quarters and down the shadowy corridor. She tried to keep note of where they were going, but there were so many twists and turns, she knew she would never be able to find her way back. She certainly wouldn't be able to find the prisoner cells without help.

They entered a large room with a ten-foot high ceiling and torches lining the walls. Ahead of her was an altar with a large fire burning in a rounded hearth. And there, standing in front of the altar, Sovold waited for her. He was flanked by two others she did not know. He no longer wore the animal skins of his tribe. Now he was dressed in the same type of uniform as Nyan and his people. His hair was combed and cleaned, his boots glossed to a high sheen. He ran his tongue over his dry lips at the sight of her.

She and Nyan paused inside the main threshold. Several more men filed in from a side entrance on the left side of the room. They joined Sovold at the altar.

~ ⧖ ~

Dane slid from the table, his feet landing on the floor with a thump. He tested the strength of his ankle and was surprised to find he had no pain, as if he'd never sprained the ankle. Whatever potion Ilsa had given him must have indeed renewed his strength, as she'd promised. He certainly felt strong, like he was whole again. He looked at the old woman, who paused at the doorway.

"Thanks," he said. "I don't know how I can repay you."

"Save the girl, that's how," she said. "One last thing." She turned, removed a package from a nearby shelf and tossed it to him. "Put that on. It will alleviate any suspicions. Follow the corridor to the dead end and then go left. The ceremony will take place in the old chapel at the end of the hallway. Now I must take my leave before I'm missed."

Dane peeled back the paper wrapping on the package and found a uniform like Nyan's inside. Before he could thank Ilsa again, however, she had disappeared from the room. Dane quickly stripped and put on the uniform. He took care to place the time bender securely in his shirt pocket and buttoned the flap. He slid the dagger into his boot instead of his belt and wished he had his gun.

He hurried out of the room that had almost been his death chamber. He would get even with Sovold for everything—trying to kill him and trying to control Skye. He slipped through the deserted corridors unnoticed and found the chapel easily, guarded by two sentries flanking the doorway. Pausing, he ducked behind a corner, pressing his back against the cold wall. He would have to kill both to get inside. He knew they wouldn't let him pass without a commotion.

He slid the dagger from his boot and crept through the shadows.

~ ⧖ ~

Skye recoiled in horror as she was led toward the altar and Sovold. How could she willingly marry that disgusting man? She had to find a way out of this because she knew there was no way she could face what happened *after* the marriage ceremony. A sick feeling crept into her throat.

Nyan gave Skye a shove toward her future husband. She stumbled, regained her footing and turned to glare at him. Again, she tried to figure out why he was doing this. Why was the leader of an obviously superior race so willing to bow to the demands of a primitive enemy?

"Do you have the treaty?" Nyan asked.

It couldn't be only about peace. There had to be something more, something Sovold had over him.

Sovold held up a scroll of parchment paper for Nyan to see. "Give me the girl first. I will give you the treaty when the ceremony is complete."

"That was not part of the plan, Sovold, and you know it," Nyan growled.

"If you do not like these terms, I can destroy it." Sovold held the scroll over the flames.

Skye glanced at Nyan, saw his jaw muscles flex as he gritted his teeth. She held her breath, waiting to see what he would say and how he would handle this new turn of events. She was hoping he would demand the treaty first, and then she would initiate her plan of action.

"As you wish then," Nyan said finally. "The ceremony first."

"No!" Skye cried, her eyes wide. Her heart thudded a loud, frightened cadence in her chest. "I will not do this."

She shook her head, tried to step back, but couldn't. She was suddenly flanked by guards who grabbed her by the arms and dragged her toward Sovold. "No, please, don't do this, Nyan!"

"Get the elixir!" Sovold ordered.

"I will not do this!" she shouted. "Let go of me!"

She flailed, kicking her legs and trying desperately to wrench her arms from the guards' grasp. They held tightly, refusing to release her.

"Get control of her, now," Nyan snapped. "Tie her up if you have to."

Another guard stepped forward, grabbed her wrists and quickly bound them. She continued to kick and flail, trying to aim for him as he lashed her wrists together. Nyan backhanded her hard across the mouth, knocking the wind out of her.

"You can do this the hard way, my dear," he said. "Or you can cooperate and save yourself a lot of trouble. Which will it be?"

She tasted the metallic tang of blood on her lip and spat at him. "I would rather burn in hell than marry Sovold."

Nyan unsheathed his sword.

"So be it."

~ ⧗ ~

Dane moved from the shadows and grabbed the first guard from behind, slitting his throat and easing his cumbersome weight to the ground to keep him silent. The second guard saw his fellow guardsman go down and reached for his sword. Placing his dagger in his belt, Dane lunged forward to meet him.

He and the guard collided, and Dane shoved him backward into the metal wall with a loud thump. He knew if he didn't take care of this one quickly, he would attract attention. The guard fumbled for his sword as Dane wrapped his hands around his throat. He clamped his palms firmly against the man's windpipe and squeezed. The man-made tiny choking sounds and pawed at Dane's hands.

He drew his leg up and kneed Dane in the groin. Grunting, he doubled over, releasing his grasp on the man's throat. His opponent unsheathed his sword and in one lightning-quick motion, Dane snatched his dagger and hurled it. The knifepoint met its target—directly in the guard's heart. His face registered surprise before he crumpled to the floor.

Dane took the guard's sword, retrieved his dagger and sheathed it in his boot, then entered the chapel. He saw Skye flailing at the front of the room, her hands tied as Nyan backhanded her across the mouth. Anger surged through Dane and he clutched the blade tighter in his sweaty grasp. He watched as Nyan removed his sword and held it to Skye's throat.

"Step away from her now," Dane said through clenched teeth.

~ ⧗ ~

Skye froze. She knew that deep, resonant voice. It was Dane. Her savior.

And he was angry. She could hear it in his words. Relief flooded through her as she craned her neck to see him. She had to see if he was all right. The sight of his bloody, swollen face shocked her. He strode forward as though his ankle no longer pained him. He was no longer limping. He looked frightful standing under the bright light, the sword in one hand and a look of pure, murderous rage on his badly beaten face.

He'd come for her.

Still holding the sword point at her throat, Nyan fixed a cold, hard glare on Dane. "You dare interrupt?"

"He is the healer and a traitor!" Sovold exclaimed. "Kill him now!"

"Hold," Nyan ordered. He looked at his men. "Do you follow me or the savage?"

"This man is dangerous." Sovold stepped down from the altar, his fists clenched.

"Then why, Sovold, was he allowed to live?" Nyan turned his gaze to the other man. "Perhaps you are not as powerful as I thought if you cannot kill a prisoner. You should have taken care of him when you had the chance."

"I would have, had it not been for—"

"No one has to get hurt," Dane interrupted, his voice calm and cool. "All I want is the girl."

Skye couldn't help but smile.

"She is worth more to me than you," Sovold said. "And I will have her for my own."

"Then I'll fight you for her," Dane said matter-of-factly. At his words, her heart kicked into a wild beat. He'd promised to protect her, no matter what. Now, he was proving it.

"Release her, Nyan."

"Never," Nyan said. And then to his soldiers, he said, "Kill him now."

As the guards turned to face Dane, Sovold grabbed Skye, jerking her roughly toward him. She twisted in his grasp, struggling against him.

"Hang on, Skye!" Dane shouted from across the room. He suddenly found himself facing a horde of guards with their swords drawn. His mind whirled, reviewing all of his mercenary training, trying to remember what he knew of sword-fighting.

Jack-shit was the best he could come up with. Daggers, somewhat. Switchblades, yes. Brass knuckles, fine and dandy, but swords? He was a bodyguard, not a damn pirate. He'd always favored a pistol for his hits and fervently wished he had his Glock.

A guard swung at him. Instinct told him to put up the sword he'd taken from the guard in the hallway in defense. Metal blade clashed against metal blade. One man would be no match against several and he had to think quickly. He felt the guard push against him, forcing him back. Their blades locked together in a glittering X almost directly in front of his face.

Dane knew he had to reach his dagger. With what strength he had, he gave the guard a furious shove. The force surprised even Dane as the guard went flying backward, landing on the floor with a resounding thud.

Ilsa had said the potion she had given him was for strength. She wasn't kidding. Whatever it was, he felt as strong as an ox, like he really could take on the guards, swords and all. Clutching his own blade tighter in his hand, Dane faced them head-on.

A sudden rumbling shook the chapel, and Dane stumbled. It was just like before, the same type of explosion he felt before when he was about to be injected with the poison. A blinding flash sent him backpedaling, and Ilsa appeared at his side.

"Ilsa?" Dane asked, startled. "What the hell are you doing here?"

"Helping you," she replied.

Nyan seemed equally surprised to see the old woman in the middle of the fray. "*Maman?*"

"Stand aside, my son," she said.

"*Maman*, I must insist—"

"Your time of insistence is over, my son," she interrupted. Then to Dane, she said: "Get the girl before the barbarian does something that is irreversible."

~ ⧖ ~

On the other side of the room, Sovold was busy trying to force Skye to drink the potion and she was refusing.

"Hold her!" he ordered.

One of his henchmen grabbed her bound arms, but she kicked wildly, aiming for Sovold's crotch. She missed, and the toe of her kidskin boot caught the edge of the glass vial he held. It flew from his hand, went up in the air end over end.

"No!" she heard him cry as the vial went airborne.

She could only hope it would land and shatter. The man holding her released her and dove, hands cupped to catch the runaway vial. Skye knew if he caught it, she'd be forced to drink whatever vile concoction it contained. And she doubted it was anything good for her.

She did the only thing she could think to do. She jumped on the soldier's back, grabbed a fistful of hair with both hands, and yanked his head back as hard as she could. He let out a loud scream that echoed off the walls around them.

The glass vial landed on the floor beyond the reach of his hands, bounced, and rolled several feet away. Sovold growled, annoyed, and picked up Skye, his hands under her armpits. His large muscular arms wrapped around her and held her tight. She could hear his heavy breath in her ear. Worse, she could smell his rancid panting. Sovold's man clambered up and snatched the vial.

"A feisty one, you are," Sovold murmured. "I like that. You'll make a good bedmate."

She stomped on the arch of his foot. He growled again but held fast. She slammed her foot down again and again, but he refused to let go. She wiggled in his grasp, trying to free herself, but couldn't.

Sovold's man now had the vial and uncorked it. Holding her in one powerful arm, Sovold reached for her jaw and squeezed her cheeks until he forced her mouth open.

"Now, pretty one, you will be mine."

~ ⧗ ~

From across the room, Dane saw Skye's peril. He couldn't get there fast enough, no matter how he tried. He slashed the guard in front of him and reached for his dagger. He hurled it through the air with precision and speed. The dagger found its mark, landing in the neck of Sovold's soldier. As the guard staggered and fell, the vial slipped from his grasp and landed at Skye's feet, spilling the liquid inside all over the floor.

"*No!*" Sovold shouted. He released Skye and bent, trying to salvage the potion. There was nothing left but broken glass and damp stone floor tiles, however, so Sovold snatched the dagger from the dead guard's neck. Standing, he grabbed Skye once more and placed the point at her throat.

"Let her go, Sovold," Dane said.

"Never," he breathed. He backed away from the altar, heading toward a side exit. "She is mine." He disappeared with Skye through the exit.

"Like hell she is."

Dane took off after them.

Chapter 7
Up the Mountain

Dane ran through the exit of the old chapel and plunged into darkness. It stopped him short. He hadn't expected it to be dark. He reached out for the wall, felt the cold metal. He strained his ears, heard the shuffling of feet and Skye's whimpering coming from somewhere ahead of him.

Despite the darkness, he charged after them. Ahead, he thought he could make out a dim pinprick of daylight. Suddenly shapes formed in the light and he knew it was Sovold and Skye. With the sword still gripped in his hand, he dashed for them, running hard and fast. All the while, the hint of light grew larger and brighter until he could make out the opening of a doorway. Sunlight reflected on newly fallen snow, blinding him.

He was sweating by the time he burst into the frigid air, his booted feet crunching on the snow-covered ground. He stopped, shaded his eyes and saw footsteps in the snow, impressions heading off directly ahead of him toward the horizon. Sovold was taking her to the mountains. There was no time to waste.

~ ⧗ ~

Skye's hands were still bound as she stumbled after Sovold. He had her arm clenched in his hand as he dragged her up the mountainside. He paused only long enough for her to catch her breath, giving her a hard shove to the frozen ground. The altitude was getting to her and she wasn't sure how much longer she could stand it. She noticed then his eyes were fixed on a structure at the top of the peak.

She squinted against the bright daylight. The sun all but blotted out the brilliant blue sky. A small building perched on the edge of the mountain he seemed intent on climbing.

"Where are we going?" she panted. She had to ask, even though she wasn't sure she wanted to know the answer.

"We go to the top," he replied, matter-of-factly. "Where you will help me get what I want."

She didn't understand what he meant, but a sickening dread coursed through her at his words. She shivered, from the cold and fear. Goosebumps rose across her half-naked body. She wore only the skimpy suede dress and boots Nyan had given her for the wedding. If the altitude sickness didn't kill her, hypothermia would. Dane was her only hope now.

"You're a fool, Sovold." Her own venomous words surprised her.

His head snapped toward her, his glare dark and frightening. She resisted the urge to gulp and forced herself to stare right back, trying gallantly to stand her ground and be brave. He squatted down in front of her and placed the cold metal blade of his bloodstained dagger alongside her cheek.

"Mind your tongue," he warned. "Or I shall cut it out. What I have planned for you does not require you to have it."

She gasped as Sovold jerked her to her feet again and they began the long trudge up once more.

A sudden rumbling of the earth beneath his feet gave Dane pause. He spun where he stood, his breath exhaling in white plumes on the frigid air. With a thunder of heavy hooves, hundreds of horses suddenly crested the nearest ridge, racing toward him. He recognized Nyan in the center, flanked by a riderless horse and Ilsa. His men rode behind them. Nyan came to a stop, his horses' hooves kicking up snow.

"Stranger, you go to save the girl." Nyan's gaze focused on Dane. It was a statement, not a question.

"Yes." Dane still gripped the sword in his hand, wondering what the chieftain was up to.

"Because she is your mate?"

His mate? "Not my mate. I swore to protect her."

True, he'd promised William Ransom he'd keep her safe. True, he'd promised he'd see her home once again. Promises he intended to keep.

Nyan and Ilsa exchanged a glance. Some silent communication passed between them.

"There is more to this *troskian* ceremony the girl does not know. In order for the prophecy of peace to come true, there must be a sacrifice."

The back of Dane's neck tingled. "What kind of sacrifice?"

"*A woman with hair the color of flame will drop from the sky. She will be the Pure One, the one who can bring peace to all the clans with her flaming death,*" Nyan said. "There is an old temple at the top of the mountain that is said to have magical powers. He intends to burn her."

He stared at him, his gut twisted. "And that woman is Skye?"

"Is she not named for the heavens?"

"Burning her alive won't give you peace. All it will do is kill an innocent woman." Anger and fear pulsed through him.

Nyan slowly nodded. "I agree. It is why I offer you a truce. Join us and we can help each other. You can save your woman and I can rid us of that vile savage."

Dane's gaze flickered between Nyan and his mother. She gave him a nod of approval, her expression urging him to mount the horse.

"We must stop Sovold before he reaches the temple," Nyan said and pointed to the building on top of the mountain.

"Then you'll free us," Dane said. "Me and the girl—both of us. We go free when it's over."

"Agreed," Nyan said quickly. He offered Dane the reins of the riderless horse beside him. "Now come before it's too late."

~ ⧗ ~

Sovold shoved Skye to the snowy ground again. She panted, her lungs burning as she tried to catch her breath. He dragged her for what seemed like hours. Her legs ached from the exertion.

"Rest." He didn't even seem winded. He paced back and forth in front of her, carving a rut in the snow. She could see the brown earth emerging beneath the heavy treads of his boots.

She glanced around, back down the way they'd come. Maybe she could make a run for it. If she was fast enough, she could get away, find Dane, and then they could use the time bender and leave this place behind. The seventy-two hours were definitely up.

"It will do you no good to try and run from me," he said, as though he'd read her thoughts. Sovold waved the dagger at her. "And I will not hesitate to kill you if you try. There is no escape for you, girl. No rescue. Not even the healer—your precious love—can save you."

"My precious…?" Skye nearly laughed aloud, despite the circumstances and her shortness of breath. He thought she and Dane were *in love*? Please.

True, Dane was hired by her father to protect her. True, she'd grown to trust him and depend on him. And true, he had an arrogant, chauvinistic attitude she could simultaneously loathe and appreciate. But that was the extent of her feelings for the man.

Sort of.

"I don't understand why you won't let me go." Her voice was weak and weary. She was so very cold. Her teeth chattered. She folded her arms in front of her trying to ward off the frigid air. It was useless, though. "Why are you doing this?"

"Because you are the Pure One." He paused, looking at her with a wicked smile and a frightful gleam in his eyes.

She stared at him, wondering what the hell that meant. She was far from pure, especially after a few shots of tequila.

"What does that mean?" She breathed the words between her teeth, her breath exhaling on a white plume.

Sovold squatted in front of her. "I knew it the moment I saw you, when I brought you and your companion to our camp. It was the color of your hair and your eyes that confirmed it." His hand slipped under her hairline, caressing the nape of her neck. "The prophecy spoke of a copper-haired woman with indigo eyes who would drop from the sky. I sensed something ancient about you. I sensed your pureness."

She flushed. Her skin tingled where he touched her and she didn't like it one bit.

"The temple, you see, is where the power lies." He pointed to the building on top of the mountain. "The prophecy states the Pure One will harness the power for the one who would proclaim himself leader and provide everlasting peace. That is why we must join together in an ancient ritual at the temple. I had thought to control you with the elixir. It would have been easier for us both. However, you insisted on kicking it from my hand."

His hand traveled down her neck. Repulsed by his touch, bile rose in her throat, but she forced it down. He gripped her hair, tilted her head back with a yank and hovered over her. She could see his stumps of yellow teeth as his lips parted and his acrid breath pressed against her face.

Oh, God. He was going to kiss her.

Nothing she'd suffered to that point—not running away from an armed hit man, traveling through time or finding herself in the middle of not one, but *numerous* major, bloody battles in the span of little more than a week—horrified her more than this sudden realization.

Panic seized her. Her hand fumbled against the snowy ground, her fingertips curling about the jagged curve of a loose rock. She swung it in her hand, smashing it into the side of his head.

Sovold grunted with the paint but released his hold on her, his hand going to his temple. She was pleased to see she had left a bright red mark and a tiny trickle of blood slipped down the side of his face. She shoved him away and scrambled to her feet, starting to run. The snow was thick and deep, however, and her boot soles slipped for clumsy purchase as she plodded forward. She didn't make it five full strides before Sovold caught her again, grabbing her roughly by the elbow. He pointed the dagger at her throat, the tip jabbing her skin.

"I should kill you now."

"Go ahead," she taunted. "I dare you."

She was banking on the fact he needed her alive for when they arrived at the temple. She held her breath, saw the flicker of indecision in his eyes and then he lowered the dagger.

"Another misstep, pretty one, and I will."

And she knew he was telling her the truth.

Chapter 8
Pure One

Dane followed Nyan's lead and spurred his horse to a gallop, his breath frosting in the thin air. Nyan and his soldiers headed toward a ridge east of the compound. The thunder of the horses' hooves was nearly deafening. Clods of snow and dirt flew up behind them as they trampled the new-fallen powder.

As they neared the ridge, a shout rose up and men and women wearing heavy furs appeared, surging over the rocky summit, running toward the cavalry. They all had spears readied, aiming their deadly points toward Nyan and his men.

"Nyan—" Dane began.

"I see them!" Nyan shouted. "Ready swords!"

He brandished his blade and his men followed suit, bellowing loud, hoarse war cries. Dane gripped his own sword tightly in his fist. He swallowed hard, his throat clenching. In his entire life, he had never faced something so intimidating. Even his military background could not prepare him for this.

Now more than ever, he needed that whiskey.

~ ⏳ ~

Sovold paused when he heard the rising shout of war cries. He smiled, cocking his head to the side. "Listen, pretty one."

She shivered next to him, her teeth chattering. She was sure her lips were blue. All she could think about was how cold she was, nothing more. She eyed the heavy jacket he wore, wondering how she could overpower him to get it. There had to be some way...

"Do you hear that?" He turned to her, genuinely interested in a response. "My people are attacking, as I knew they would."

"A-attacking?" she stuttered, coming out of her trance. Detaching her mind from her current situation was the only way she could hope to survive. What was he talking about?

"My clansmen. I knew that fool Nyan would attempt to follow me when he realized where I was headed. They will detain him, giving us enough time to reach the temple."

He turned and headed back up the mountain, pulling her along behind him.

"D-dane…where are you?" she whispered.

Sovold's fingers dug into her arm, but the pressure no longer hurt her. She couldn't feel anything. Her entire body was leaden and numb with cold. Her wrists were still bound. The ropes had rubbed her raw. She knew she was losing strength and if she didn't do something soon, she would have hypothermia and frostbite. Her vision blurred and she stumbled. Sovold held tight, jerking her up to keep her on her feet.

"Come on, girl," he growled.

She saw something glinting in the bright morning sunlight. It was the dagger. He held it carelessly in his other hand. Her mind, even dazed, tried to come up with a way to kick it out of his hand, get it, and then turn it on him. She needed his jacket and desperately.

He took a sharp turn to the left to avoid large boulders jutting out of the side of the mountain. Now was her chance.

As he continued to veer to the left, steering them closer to the boulders, Skye used what strength she had remaining to jerk to the right. She slammed her frozen body into the boulder, jarring her senses. Leaning into the cold rock, she kicked with both feet, landing her blows onto Sovold. It was a feeble attempt, but enough to cause him to stumble. She could feel his grip on her loosen a bit.

He started to fall and she knew he would take her with him. Her hands were already at work, twisting and turning, trying to get free of the ropes. As he fell, his hand slipped off her arm. He landed and rolled several feet down the slope, while she crumpled into a heap in the snow.

Looking up, she saw the glint of the dagger. He had dropped it on his tumble. Skye crawled toward it. Her bleeding wrists throbbed. She couldn't feel her arms or hands. She couldn't feel anything. All she knew was she had to get that knife. She was covered in snow by the time she got there. She clasped her hand around it, feeling triumphant.

But it didn't last long. Sovold's booted foot stomped down, pinning her raw wrists to the ground.

"Not so fast, my pretty."

~ ⧗ ~

On the other side of the ridge, Dane spied the two people heading slowly up the hill before they disappeared around the boulders. He recognized Skye's half-naked form and Sovold's ugly profile even from a distance.

"There they are." He pointed at the couple along the mountainside.

Nyan hadn't heard him. He was busy with one of the attackers. He slashed one of the savage men, cutting him nearly in half. The man screamed, crumpling to the ground. All around Dane could hear the clash of swords, the grunts of men killing each other, and the air was thick with the metallic tang of freshly spilled blood.

One of Sovold's tribesmen grabbed for his horse's reins as Dane kicked his horse, trying to spur it in Skye's pursuit. Another tried to climb on the back of the saddle. Dane cut down the one at the reins, while his horse whinnied in protest and reared back. Holding on tightly, Dane did his best not to fall off of the beast.

Another one of the savages jumped on the horse and his massive arms wrapped around the animal's neck. He was using his weight to try and pull the horse down. Dane knew if he succeeded, he could be pinned under the powerful animal.

"Dane!"

He heard the voice, aware someone was nearby. He recognized Ilsa, who galloped toward him.

"Do not move," she ordered.

A booming clap of thunder shook the air and ground alike, and a bright flash of light momentarily dazzled Dane. The savages trying to take him down fell to the ground in a lifeless heap. Dane opened his eyes warily and glanced at Ilsa, who sat still and straight in her saddle. The small woman, it seemed, was a ball of energy and power.

"You've saved me once again, Ilsa." He smiled broadly.

"You may express your thanks later. Right now, you must hurry. Get to the girl before it's too late." She pointed toward the mountains.

Grabbing his horse's reins in one hand and griping his bloodied sword in the other, Dane galloped toward Skye and Sovold.

~ ⧗ ~

Skye whimpered. It was the only sound that would come out of her constricted throat. Fear was a terrible thing, she thought, as she glanced into the frightening face of Sovold. He hadn't moved his foot. Instead he crushed her wrists into the ground. This time she screamed.

"I suppose I will have to carry you to the temple in pieces." He kneeled down to her level and brushed her hair out of her eyes. "A pity, too. You are so lovely. I hate to mar your face."

He reached for the dagger and tugged it away from her hands, brushing the clumps of snow from it. He held it, turning it to and fro so the morning sunlight glinted off of the bloodstained blade.

"Sovold," she began weakly. "You don't need to do that. I'll cooperate."

"Oh, but that time has passed, pretty one." He brushed the cold metal against her skin. "You had your chance."

"Please," she said, hunching her shoulders and cowering. "I can be reasonable."

"I do not believe you can."

The blade was on her cheekbone now. He applied a slight pressure and she felt the bite of the knife edge into her skin. She jerked her head to the side, away from him. He emitted a low guttural growl. His free hand went to the back of her neck, pressing her face into the snow. He placed the blade back on her cheek. Then, as an afterthought, he moved it to the corner of her eye at her temple.

"Perhaps I'll take your eyesight from you now, since you are so troublesome." His free hand knotted in her hair. "Or perhaps a little pain will force you into submission."

She sobbed openly now. He was going to kill her before Dane could reach them. Her tears felt like frozen icicles on her face. The blade pierced her delicate skin as he dragged it down the length of her face. She screamed, an agonized, terrified howl escaping her lungs as the razor edge sliced her face open from temple to chin. The cold air hit the open wound, sending a chill through her blood.

Then he stopped, the dagger moving away from her face. Through the haze of her tears, she saw him look into the distance.

She felt and heard something. Could it be? The ground rumbled under her. She strained her ears, heard the thudding and rhythmic beating of a horse's hooves.

"No!" Sovold shouted. "It cannot be!"

Releasing her quickly, he shot to his feet. She clawed the snow as she crawled away from him. She saw a man riding furiously toward them on horseback—his dark hair unmistakable, his icy green eyes blazing with anger and hatred. He brandished a bloodstained sword high above his head in one hand and in the other, the reins of the horse.

In a daze, she realized it was Dane.

Relief sputtered through her hazy brain as she huddled against the boulder. Her hands, legs and arms were numb. Her face streamed blood. The man sworn to protect her pulled his mount to a stop and jumped from the saddle in one fluid motion.

~ ⧗ ~

Dane paused in front of Sovold, his sword gripped tightly in his hand. Sovold had only the dagger for defense.

"Get away from her, you son of a bitch," Dane growled.

"I am impressed with your resourcefulness," Sovold said, coolly. "You are still alive when you should be dead."

"I'm here for the girl," Dane said, ignoring him. "Now get away from her before I kill you."

"My people have failed me once again," Sovold said. "But that will not stop me from getting to the temple. You may try to kill me, healer, but you will not succeed."

"Watch me," Dane said. "I have a sword. You don't."

Sovold stared at him in silence, gripping the bloodied dagger in his hand. He looked thoughtful a moment. Dane watched him with a keen eye, waiting for his next move. He held his breath, unaware of the cold around him. His gaze flickered to Skye hovering on the ground against the boulder, shivering, her lips blue, and her face bloodied.

Sovold lunged at Dane while his guard was down, while he

was distracted looking at Skye. Sovold slashed Dane's wrist, causing him to drop the sword, and then crashed into him. The two men tumbled to the ground and tussled together, rolling several feet until Sovold ended up on top.

The tip of his dagger was in Dane's face, a breath away from his eyes. Dane held on to Sovold's wrist, pushing him back with what precious remaining strength he had, but he could feel it waning. Sovold, on the other hand, seemed to have summoned up some hidden reserve. He was like an ox and he wasn't sure how much longer he could keep him at bay.

~ ⧖ ~

Skye watched, horrified, as the dagger came closer and closer to Dane's face. Her mind was weary, but she knew she had to do something to help him. She knew she had to act before her only potential savior was killed. She glanced around, searching for something—anything—to use as a weapon. The only things her hands found were rocks.

Although her wrists were still bound, she managed to grasp one in her hands. She wasn't sure what kind of aim she would have, but she had to try. Clutching the rock and a handful of snow, she struggled to her feet. She couldn't hit him at this distance. She needed to be closer.

Stumbling, she nearly fell, but caught herself. She was close now and, with both hands, she tossed the rock as hard as she could at Sovold. It smacked him on the back of his head. He grunted, momentarily dazed and rolled off Dane.

Weak, Skye collapsed and tried to crawl away. She had lost her strength, unable to sit upright. She watched, though, her mind numb and nearly gone, as Dane rolled on top of Sovold, his hands clamping around the man's thick neck.

She noticed the dagger then, lying in the snow near the struggling men. If she could get to it, she could help. She started to crawl toward them, her eyes never leaving the knife.

As she wiggled through the snow, though, she heard new thunder. She looked up, saw more horses and hoped that was help on the way and not the fellow clansmen Sovold had told her about.

Pausing, she watched them ride closer and realized she was in danger of being trampled. Dane was too busy with Sovold to help her out of this one. She started scrambling away, toward the boulder, toward safety.

~ ⧗ ~

Dane's hands were around Sovold's meaty neck, his fingers pushing as hard as he could into the other man's flesh. Sovold's eyes bulged slightly, he gasped for air, trying to breathe. His legs were kicking, his hands clawing at Dane's to try and release his grip.

But Dane held fast. He was aware of the dagger nearby but didn't want to release Sovold to reach for it. He wanted to keep his hands firmly planted on Sovold's neck because he was going to make sure the savage never laid a hand on Skye again.

In his peripheral vision, he saw her collapse in the snow, and then try to scramble toward him. He realized she was going for the knife. She meant to try and help him. Damn her. He was supposed to be rescuing her, not the other way around. He wanted to shout to her to stop, to get away, but the rumbling of the horses cut him short. Skye heard them, too, and scrambled away, he hoped, to safety.

Sovold gasped for breath one last time, his eyes turning lifeless, as Nyan and his men galloped into view. Nyan jumped from his mount and hurried over. Dane removed his cramping hands from Sovold's neck and sat back, staring down at the man's blue face.

"You have killed the leader," Nyan stated, his voice cold and unfeeling.

"Justice." Dane struggled to his feet and turned, found Skye passed out face-down in the snow. "Skye!"

He ran to her, knelt at her side and scooped her into his arms. He held her frigid body close to his, brushing away strands of auburn hair from her bloodied cheek, then felt for a pulse. It was faint, but apparent. She was still alive.

"Skye, can you hear me?"

"Maman!" Nyan shouted.

Ilsa was already out of her saddle and hurrying toward them. She dropped to her knees next to Skye and Dane. "The savage nearly killed her. I can help her, but she is close to death."

Ilsa put a hand on Skye's forehead and reached into her pouch. She pulled out a handful of what looked like sparkling sand. She sprinkled it over Skye and chanted in her native tongue. As Dane held her, her body warmed and then saw the blinding white flash that he had come to associate with Ilsa. The light was so bright he had to turn his head and squeeze his eyes shut.

A moment later, all was quiet. A stillness had fallen. Dane looked down at Skye. The wound on her face, while not completely healed, was closed and only a smattering of dried blood remained. She sucked in a sudden sharp breath and her eyes fluttered open.

Her color had returned. Her lips were no longer blue. She didn't even shiver in his arms. He was amazed she didn't have frost bite or hypothermia, especially with the skimpy outfit that barely covered her.

Long milky white legs ended in fur-lined boots. The dress, it seemed, hugged her body, showing off all the right curves in all the right places. He was so relieved she was all right, he pulled her against him, hugging her.

"It's all right now, Skye. It's over. You're safe."

Chapter 9
Victory Celebration

She blinked, looking up at him. "Why does this keep happening to me?"

He chuckled, brushing away a lock of hair. "Maybe it's your winning personality."

She mustered up enough strength to stick out her tongue at him.

As he grinned at her childish response, his gaze met hers. Something happened then as they looked at each other. The shaky breath she exhaled plumed white between them and somehow, she knew...*knew*...he was going to kiss her.

And unlike when Sovold threatened to do the same, she was not revolted by the idea. A tingling sense of anticipation and desire and need flickered through her at the very thought of him kissing her and suddenly it was the only thing she ever wanted. Her lips parted as his head dipped toward hers and then—

"Looks as though the little one will be okay."

Ilsa's voice snapped the magical spell surrounding the two of them. Dammit.

Dane's head snapped up. It might have been her imagination, but she was certain she could see the rapid beat of his pulse in the column of his neck.

Fist pump.

Skye turned her head to see the elderly woman sitting beside them, her brow winkled in concern.

"Hey, Ilsa."

"You've met?" Dane asked, and Skye nodded.

Skye nodded. "When Nyan dressed me up like a doll." She waved at the outfit and rolled her eyes. Skye then reached for her cheek, placing fingers against the newly healed wound. "I don't get it. How…?"

"I have healed you," she said. She placed a gnarled hand on her shoulder. "How do you feel, child?"

"Better and, strangely, warm."

How as that possible? Only moments ago, she thought she might freeze to death.

Did it have something to do with being cradled in Dane's arms? She dismissed the silly thought. No way could he have any feelings. Likely, her warmth-deprived brain imagined he was going to kiss her. He was older and probably wanted someone more mature and that wasn't her.

But then, she thought she could feel the swift beat of his heart through his borrowed uniform. Or was that simply her overactive imagination?

"Sovold is dead," Nyan announced. "As are most of his clansmen. The rest are in my custody."

"What will happen to them?" Dane asked.

"They will remain prisoners," Nyan said. "Perhaps peace has been achieved at last."

"We should get your woman inside." Ilsa rose, brushed snow from her skirts. "Before she starts to feel cold again. The healing spell will not last forever."

Dane stood, helping Skye to her feet. He still held her close, his arm around her shoulders. It was as though he refused to leave her side.

Nyan picked up the dagger, then sliced the rope from Skye's wrists. He removed his fur from his shoulders and held it out to her. "I would be honored, my lady, if you would take this to help keep you warm."

Gratefully, she took it and wrapped it around her shoulders. It was still warm from his body heat and she relished it. "Thank you," she said sincerely.

"It would be my privilege if you both would join me this evening in a feast to honor your acts of bravery," Nyan said. "You are welcome here as our guests for as long as you would like to stay."

"Thanks, but we need to be going," Dane said.

"After the feast, of course," Skye said, elbowing him in the ribs. She looked at him. "I'm starving, you know. I feel like I haven't eaten in millennia."

~ ⧗ ~

The group headed back down the mountainside to the compound. Skye rode with Dane, bundled against him on horseback. Her small body was warm against his as they rode down the mountainside. She seemed content.

"How's your ankle?" She gave him a glance over her shoulder.

"Healed by Ilsa. She is…" He paused, unable to voice the words.

Skye turned her head to peer at him. "Magic?"

He nodded. "Is that crazy?"

She faced forward again. "No. Something happened in the chapel with her, too. Didn't it?"

"Yes, something I can't explain. She wanted to help me when Nyan didn't. She wanted me to save you from Sovold. Why would she do that?" he asked.

"I don't know but I'm glad she did. This place is strange, Dane. I'm not sure how they ended up here with two societies so far from each other," Skye said. "It makes me wonder about…"

"About?"

"Are we changing the timeline?"

"I don't know but we can't worry about that. All we need to worry about is trying to get home."

"That reminds me. You still have the time bender, right?"

"Fear not, princess. It's safe with me."

He couldn't tell her the relief he felt when she awoke in his arms. Or that he actually did consider kissing her if Ilsa hadn't interrupted. And why was he thinking that, anyway? She wasn't his type. Far from it.

"Dane…do you think we'll make it back?"

"I hope so, Skye. I really do."

~ ⧗ ~

When they arrived back at the compound, Nyan proved true to his word and ordered an enormous feast to celebrate their triumph. Skye and Dane went their separate ways. He was led to his own room while she was taken to the room she'd occupied before. She enjoyed a long, hot shower and changed into less conspicuous attire. Nyan provided her with boots, suede pants and a pull-over sweater. She pulled her freshly-washed hair back into a ponytail and secured it with a leather thong at the nape of her neck.

A knock sounded on the door before it opened. Ilsa entered the room, a smile on her aged face.

"You look lovely, my dear."

"Thanks. That shower did the trick."

"I've come to take you to the dining hall." She waved toward the door.

As they walked through the corridors, Skye said, "Thank you for your help with Sovold."

"It was the right thing to do. Those savages have been a problem for a while now. Hopefully, peace will finally be obtained."

"I hope so, too."

As they entered the dining hall, savory aromas filled the air. Her stomach rumbled in response. Dane sat with Nyan and a few others. He saw her enter and their eyes locked. He'd cleaned up and shaved as well and had ditched the uniform. Now he wore a black long-sleeved shirt and black pants. Perhaps he hadn't meant to, but he looked her up and down and then smiled. Heat pushed into her cheeks.

When the two women approached, the men got to their feet.

"Come, Skye. Sit here next to me and my *maman*." He waved to the open seat next to him.

She passed by Dane, acutely aware he never took his gaze off her. She took her seat and the others followed. In the center of the long table were serving dishes of roasted meats, vegetables, bread, fruits. Bottles of vodka and ale were passed around.

Skye had to wonder where they managed to get all this food while the savages appeared to be starving. Plus, they lived in this compound while the others lived on the frozen tundra in tents with no running water. It didn't make sense.

"Your clan appears to be more advanced that Sovold's, Nyan," Dane said, as though hearing her own questioning thoughts. "Why is that?"

"It is the way of things." Nyan popped a grape in his mouth, deeming his response answer enough.

Ilsa merely snorted.

"*Maman*—"

"What my son refuses to tell you is our bleak history," she said, interrupting him.

"Now is not the time."

"When is the time, my son? Our people know the history."

"But they are strangers here."

Skye tried not to take offense to that. She leaned forward and peered down the table at Dane who held a cup clasped tight in his hand.

"Strangers who nearly died for our cause," Ilsa said to Nyan. Then she directed her next comments to Dane. "Many long years ago, a great cloud came from the sky covering the world in darkness. The winter came and never left. Some of our people became sick, even died. Others remained healthy and learned to live off the lands. They hunted. Slowly life returned. My son and these are the third generation of survivors."

"So Sovold's men were part of those who lived off the land?" Dane asked.

"Yes," Nyan said. "They warred constantly for supremacy between them. Only a few tribes remain living out there."

By out there, Skye knew he meant on the frozen tundra.

"So why kill Odren?" She blurted the question before her brain told her not to.

All eyes landed on her. A few of the men looked astounded she had the audacity to ask such a thing. Others looked angry. Nyan narrowed his gaze at her.

"He begged for shelter because his people were dying. But I knew he and Sovold intended to kill me and take over," Nyan said.

"So, you struck first," Dane said.

"Upon my council, he did," Ilsa said.

"What about this prophecy?" Dane wanted to know. "Where does that fit?"

Nyan took a swig of vodka before answering. "The Pure One is the one who will defeat a black evil intent on taking control of the weak. It states she is a copper-haired woman who falls from the sky to save us."

Skye had felt the color drain from her face at this. Sovold had told her something very similar as he'd dragged her toward the mountaintop.

"If she cannot defeat the evil," Nyan continued. "Black evil will capture her and take her to the Temple of Power on the mountaintop. There, he will tie her to the altar and pierce her heart with a dagger to spill her blood. He will burn her on the alter while she's slowing bleeding to death to release the magic in the temple and give him ultimate power."

The black evil. Skye shivered. It seemed as good a way as any to describe Sovold.

If it hadn't been for Ilsa helping Dane to escape his bonds, then she would have surely died in that temple. He'd already started carving her face. She reached up, placed a hand against the faint scar still on her cheek.

"I wish to show you both something. Come with me." Nyan said to Skye and Dane. He rose to his full height and gestured for them to follow.

He led them outside of the compound. He walked a few feet into the dark night, his footsteps leaving a trail in the snow. They followed. Nyan pointed to the mountaintop where a large bonfire blazed against the black sky.

"We have destroyed the Temple of Power." He turned to look at the two of them. "Though I am pained to see the ancient structure burned to the ground, never again will another try to rise to power through it." He gazed pointedly at Skye. "And never again will another hurt you to claim it."

"I'm so sorry, Nyan," Skye said.

It was all she could think to say. The wind kicked up, blowing her hair in her face. He turned to face them then, a wounded look in his black eyes.

"It's the way it has to be," he said. "And I'm sorry it has come to this. In my efforts to make peace between our tribes, I nearly saw us all destroyed by that monster, Sovold."

"Why try for peace with them at all?" Skye asked. It had puzzled her all along, how doggedly Nyan had pursued a treaty with Sovold's tribe. "Your people are obviously so much more advanced than Sovold's. Why didn't you use your technology to conquer them?"

Nyan was quiet for a moment. "Because Sovold's people are mine, too. My mother, Ilsa, was born among them. Her father was a shaman and she learned her healing arts from him. But she fell in love with a soldier who happened to be my father. She left her tribe to be here with him. To conquer Sovold's tribe, to kill his people, would have been to do so to my own."

It confirmed that Skye thought about Ilsa. She hadn't imagined her use of what appeared to be magic. And, who knows, maybe it was some type of magic after all.

Nyan turned to them both, pasting on a bright smile. "Those days are behind us now and that threat has passed. Thanks to you both. Come now. We have much to celebrate and the night is still young!"

Chapter Ten
Last Man Standing

After the feast, the evening turned even more festive with music and dancing. Nyan showed off his less than serious side when he danced with reckless abandon with not only his mother—who still had moves even at her age—but with Skye, too.

She laughed and smiled until her cheeks hurt as he grasped her by the hands and whirled her in a tight circle.

"This is how we dance here." He spun her around again and she laughed. "Are you having fun?"

"A real blast," she said on a breathless laugh.

He paused twirling her and cocked his head to the side. "And this is good?"

She laughed again. "Yes."

"Mind if I cut in?" Dane had made his way to them and practically wedged himself between them.

Nyan relented, backing away. "Be my guest."

The music suddenly changed from upbeat and fast paced to slow. Dane took a step toward her, standing an inch away from her. She inhaled the heady scent of his soap as she gazed into those sharp piercing green eyes. She had never noticed how green they were until that moment.

He slid his arms around her waist and pulled her to him. His body was warm against hers and suddenly her heart started to beat wicked fast.

"Did you pay off the band to make it a slow dance?" Skye quipped.

"Just got lucky." He flashed her a fierce smile, fire flashing in his eyes.

She hadn't forgotten how he'd almost kissed her on the mountain. Nor had she forgotten she wanted him to kiss her. The way he was looking at her now though made her think he wanted to do more than kiss her.

But she had other questions on her mind and she needed answers.

"Did my father really hire you?"

"He did."

"When?"

"The day your mother died."

An instant lump formed in her throat. The same day her father was killed. Both of them taken from her on the same day. Both in the most horrific day.

Even though she didn't want to remember, she forced her mind to go back. Her mother had died in a shooting at a downtown Arlington café. When Skye couldn't reach her by phone, she went immediately to her father's office for help.

Dane had been there that day. He'd been the one in her father's office as she forced her way inside his office. Moments later her father had been gunned down.

"I don't understand. You mean you were on the job less than a day?"

"Yes."

She blinked. "So…wasn't your job fulfilled when he died?"

"No," he said, his voice low and soft.

Her heart raced. "What do you mean no?"

"He hired me to protect you, too. I intend to do just that."

"But—"

"But what, Skye? This isn't complicated. I was hired to do a job and I intend to do it." Impatience was in his voice.

They lapsed into silence as they moved around the room. If what he said was true, and she didn't doubt him, then that meant her father likely never paid him. Which meant he was doing this, what, out of the goodness of his heart? Why would he continue with a job without pay?

"What is it, Skye?"

"Nothing."

"Wrong. Your thoughts are written all over your face. What is it you want to ask me?"

She bit her lip. For a brief second, he focused on that before lifting his gaze back to hers. "If you accepted the job the day he died, then how did you get paid for it?"

He clenched his jaw. She could see the muscles working there. Finally, he said, "I didn't."

"So why do you—"

"Christ, Skye, will you shut up? You ask far too many questions."

He pulled her closer to him and their bodies meshed. They were pressed together in a way they hadn't been when they time traveled. She didn't know what to think about it. Her conflicting emotions raged within her as the music ended and they finally came to a halt. But even so, Dane seemed reluctant to release her.

"Well done, you two." Nyan clapped as he approached them. "Now, we drink!"

~ ⧗ ~

If there was one thing Skye learned was that Nyan and his people loved their vodka. They drank until the wee hours of the night while a wicked winter storm raged outside. Inside, they were all warm and toasty and mostly drunk.

As the party started to wind down, Skye decided it was a good time to make her exit. She bid everyone goodnight, not that they noticed since they were well into the bottom of a vodka bottle, and headed for her assigned room.

"I think I'll turn in, too. Can I walk with you?" Dane joined her on the way back to the private quarters.

Why did her heart leap into her throat? It didn't make sense. "Sure."

They walked in silence down the shadowy corridor. She wanted to ask him more questions about everything—from when they planned to get out of here with the time bender to why he really wanted to continue to protect her.

Her palms broke into a sudden hot sweat and she was all too aware of Dane striding in long, slow strides next to her, his booted feet near silent on the floor. She could smell a faint trace of smoked meat on his clothes and, underneath that, the bright scent of his soap or aftershave.

He walked her all the way to her door, as if they were on some kind of first date and she needed an escort. At her door, they paused. She turned to him, pasted on a smile.

"Well…goodnight, Dane."

"Goodnight." He started to turn away, then turned back. "Skye, I think this should be our last night here."

She nodded. "I agree. The time bender is safe?"

He reached into his pants pocket and pulled it out, showing it to her. "Safe."

"Good." She nodded again, feeling awkward. "We'll leave in the morning?"

"I think we should."

"Okay."

His eyes searched her face as though he wanted to say something else. Then he took a step toward her and filled up the entire space in front of her, pushing her against her door and pressing his heated body against hers. How could she object? Her head *thunked* back against the door as he leaned in and the next thing she knew he was kissing her.

His mouth landed on hers in a scorching kiss of reckless abandon. Her arms wrapped around his waist while his hands tangled in her long hair. They stood there, against her door, twined together and kissing as though they never wanted to stop. It stole her breath and robbed her of all her good sense and all she could think about was how great his mouth felt on hers, the way he tasted of a hint of smoked meat laced with vodka and the way his body pressed into hers as though he needed something more than kissing.

It was the best kiss she'd ever had in her life.

When it was over, he pressed his forehead against hers. Her breath shuddered out of her in gulps. His hands were still tangled in her hair, clutching her head between his palms as though he was reluctant to release her.

What should she do now? Invite him in for a nightcap? She was so not good at relationships or reading people and she didn't know what his expectations were.

He released her then, stepped back, smoothed his hands down his shirt front. "I'll see you in the morning."

And that was that. She watched him walk away, a sense of emptiness and disappointment flooding her.

A pounding on her door brought her out of a deep, blissful slumber. It took forever for her to fall asleep after that super-hot kiss from Dane. All she could think about was the what-if scenarios that could have played out had he not walked away.

"Skye?"

His muffled voice came through the door. She dragged her tired body out of the bed and glanced in the mirror, suddenly worried about having bedhead and her wrinkled clothes she'd slept in. She ran her fingers through her hair as he pounded on the door again.

She rushed to it and whisked it open. "Are you trying to wake the entire compound?"

"No, just you." He looked her up and down. "You sleep like the dead or something?"

"Well, I *was* but I'm not now."

"Get your stuff. Let's go." He waved her out the door.

"Stuff? What stuff? It's not like I have luggage."

"Just come on so we can get out of here before Nyan or Ilsa want to give us sappy goodbyes."

She scowled at him but followed after him. She wished she could say farewell to them since they'd been so kind, but she understood where he was coming from. There was too much to be explained. Too much that sounded like science fiction or madness.

And besides, goodbyes sucked.

They made their way out of the compound and into the bright morning light. Newly fallen snow blanketed the ground and there was a crisp, fresh smell on the cold wind. It was the perfect day for them to escape. Hopefully this time back home.

Dane took her hand, lacing his fingers with hers. They exchanged a smile. Hers of relief and hope that maybe, just maybe, they'd make it back to their time, their world. Dane paused in a clearing outside of the compound as the sun peeked over the distant mountains. Beneath the first morning rays, the snow glistened brightly. Dane reached into his pocket, grasped the time bender and handed it to her.

"You do it."

She held it in her palm for a moment, then shook her head. "No, I've pushed the button the last two times. You should have a turn."

"I'm not a toddler who needs a turn, Skye." There was a teasing twinkle in his green eyes.

She shoved it in his hand anyway. "You do it, okay?"

"If you insist." His thumb hovered over the button. "Ready?"

"I'm ready," she replied, with a nod.

The device blinked on, the green display still showing disjointed numbers. Like the LCD display had somehow been damaged.

"How do we know where we're going?" she asked.

"I guess that's a gamble we're going to have to take," he said.

A flash of light a hundred yards away caught her attention and then someone lumbered over the snow. She squinted against the morning sun trying to make out who it was, but something wasn't right. He looked…out of place from the normal inhabitants of this time.

"Is that Nyan?"

Dane caught sight of the man, too. "If it is, what is he doing out here so early?"

Sunlight glinted off something. As he neared, she could see he wore modern—from her era—snow gear. He carried a handgun and a terrible smirk on his ugly face. She'd know that face anywhere. She had nightmares about that face.

"Uh, Dane?"

"I see him—"

The hit man pointed the gun at Skye. In a reflex reaction, Dane shoved her out of the way and dove as he fired. He angled his body so his shoulder took the bullet. He crashed against the snow, blood seeping through his coat.

"Dane!"

She collapsed next to him, frantically trying to think what to do. Her hands shook as she reached for him, but he batted her away.

"I'm all right," he said through gritted teeth. "Get the time bender, Skye. Push the damn button."

"But—"

"Don't argue with me, just do it. Before he—"

A shower of bullets erupted in front of them. He'd switched the handgun for an AR-15. Skye glanced around, looking for the small device. Dane dropped it in the snow when he shoved her out of the way. She dove for it as the hit man fired again.

Her hand went around the device. She glanced up, saw him advancing on them with the rifle in hand, ready to fire. She flung her body on top of Dane's as a human shield, clutched the time bender in her hand and squeezed her eyes shut.

Skye pushed the button.

###

Skye and Dane's adventure will continue
in Volume 3: The Citadel

Sneak Peak of The Citadel, Vol 3!

Dane startled awake. As his eyes blinked open, his first sense of his surroundings was the oppressive heat and humidity. Sweat trickled down his spine. Overhead, a thick canopy of trees filtered out the sunlight. He could hear a strange cacophony of birds, beasts and other unseen animals.

His left shoulder barked in pain. The last thing he remembered was Ark Crane showing up and opening fire. He groaned and rolled to this side, shrugging out of the oversized coat and shoving it aside.

The bullet hit him in the shoulder. Blood soaked the sleeve of the borrowed uniform. He gave it a rip and pulled it off to inspect his injury. Dark blood oozed around the entry wound. He hissed with the tenderness and knew a bullet was lodged in his shoulder.

He'd been shot plenty of times but those times, he was close to modern medicine. Glancing around, it appeared they were in a jungle or rainforest and that didn't bode well. They managed to leap from one extreme to the other.

He fumbled with the material of his ripped sleeve, trying to blot the oozing blood. He didn't have anything long enough that would serve as a bandage.

A female groan reminded him he wasn't traveling solo. He glanced around the ground foliage to see Skye's copper hair peeking out from under the bracken. He scooted closer to her. A pattern of sunlight drifted over her face as she slept, her dark lashes against her face, her lips slightly parted. Her long wavy hair was splayed out around her head, littered with leaves. One arm was out to the side, the time bender resting in her palm. He leaned over to get a look at it and saw the green display still malfunctioning with the scrambled date.

Figures.

He reached for it and tucked it into his pants pocket,

wincing with the pain. He did a mental inventory of the rest of his body parts and found nothing else hurt. He was fortunate enough to land and avoid injury.

Who knew what kind of hostile natives roamed these parts? They had been lucky so far in Scotland, and then with Nyan and Ilsa. How long before their luck ran out?

Skye groaned and finally came awake. Not slowly or gently. She bolted straight up, her indigo eyes wide as she looked around and then her gaze landed on him. Relief was brief on her face before it was replaced with concern. She scooted closer to him.

"You were shot." She reached for him.

He cradled his arm to his chest and batted her hand away. "I'm shot, yes. There's nothing to do about it right now."

"We need to find a way to stop the bleeding." She looked around for something—anything—to staunch the flow. He didn't have the heart to tell her not to bother. He'd already lost a lot of blood.

"I'll be fine," he said through his teeth.

"No, you're not. You need a doctor. We have to find one."

Dane didn't answer. A doctor may be few and far between in whatever strange world they landed. He climbed to his feet, cradling his arm still, and held down his other hand to her. "We should get going. We can't stay here."

She grasped his hand and he helped haul her to her feet. She brushed away the leaves from her clothes, then shucked the heavy coat she'd worn back in winter. She dumped it on the ground in the underbrush. Then she set about getting all the leaves out of her hair. Frustration with her tangled locks was evident on her face. Her hands halted as she met his gaze.

"What?"

He hadn't realized he stared. He shook it off. She was at

least ten years his junior. She was still in college and he was well beyond those years. He shouldn't have kissed her, dammit. He wasn't sure why he had.

"Nothing. Are you hurt?"

"No." She inspected her limbs, searching for cuts and scrapes, but found none. Panic flickered over her face. "The time bender—"

"Right here." He patted his pocket.

"Eventually we're going to lose that tiny thing during one of these jumps."

He didn't disagree. It was small enough it could be easily dropped. Falling though time had proved violent and knocked them both unconscious. They needed a way to stay alert during the fall, but he didn't know how to make that happen. He was no scientist.

"Let's get moving."

"Where are we going?"

"You want to sit here in the jungle for three days?"

"Not really."

"Then we need to find some place we can blend in." He eyed her hair. "Though that may be tough to do with your hair."

She ran a hand over it, pulling out more leaves and looked offended. "What about my hair?"

How could he tell her that flame-colored hair of hers was going to make her stand out like a clown at a Ted Talk?

"Never mind."

He picked his way through the underbrush, his booted feet crunching on leaves and sticks. If only he had an idea of where and when they were, that would help them. She stumbled over a fallen log. He grasped her hand in his.

"Let me help you."

~ ⧗ ~

Skye allowed him to lace his fingers with hers, acutely aware of his roughened palm against hers. Following him through the brushy path, she kept her eyes fixed on the ground so she wouldn't stumble again. At least her feet wouldn't stumble. Her heart insisted on doing that as she focused on her hand in his. Which made her think about the searing hot kiss they'd shared back in the winter time.

She didn't want to think about the kiss, but it was at the forefront of her mind. It was permanently branded there. Why had he kissed her? Sure, they'd fallen through time together a couple of times, they were stuck with one another, but she wasn't sure there was any sort of attraction there.

Oh, who was she kidding? Dane was hot. She glanced at him as he led her through the jungle, shoving aside leaves and branches for her. His looks reminded her of Clive Owen except without the accent. He was older by at least by a decade. She didn't know much about him, other than her father hired him as protection. A lot of good that did since she was the only one in her family still alive.

"Why do you suppose the hit man wants me dead?" She blurted the words before she had time to stop them from spilling out.

"Likely because you—we—have this little time machine and they want it back."

"Who's they?"

Dane halted, his feet crunching on the bracken as he turned to look at her. "You don't know?"

"Should I?"

Thoughtful consideration flickered over his features. "I guess you wouldn't."

"Do you know?" She cocked her head to the side, her eyes narrowed to suspicious slits.

"Your father told me some, but I don't know it all."

"Care to share?"

"DARPA is involved. If DARPA is involved, it can't be good."

"What's DARPA?"

His face went blank as he processed her question. "What's DARPA?" he repeated, his tone suggesting surprise.

"That's what I asked, isn't it?"

Sweat trickled down the side of his face and beaded his forehead. He released her and swiped his hand over his damp face. "Defense Advanced Research Projects Agency."

"Oh."

She still didn't have a clue. She knew her father was former military, knew he was into some top-secret stuff, but she had no idea what he did for a living.

"What do they do?"

"They're part of the Department of Defense. They develop new technologies for use by the military."

Something about the way he said it made her bristle. "You don't have to dumb it down for me. I'm not an idiot."

The implications of her father being involved with DARPA made her spine tingle and not in a good way. She understood what it meant. She understood her father was into something deep. Maybe something so deep he couldn't get out of it. That was why he had death threats. Why he was murdered. Why her mother was murdered.

"So, you understand what it means for your father to be involved with them?"

"I know he had Top Secret security clearance, if that's what you're asking." She folded her arms over her chest. The humidity suffocated her. Sweat dripped down her back. "I know his research involved things he couldn't and didn't talk about."

"Things like a mini time machine," he said.

"Things like that, yes. Did DARPA send the hit man?"

"I don't know."

She scanned the jungle around her. Had they landed in the past, present or future? It was hard to say. "Where do you think we are?"

"The jungle."

She gave him a straight face. "I know that. *When* do you think we are?"

A loud roar sounded somewhere in the distance. Gooseflesh erupted on her arms. She stepped closer to Dane. One corner of his mouth lifted in a cocky grin, lighting up the clear green depths of his eyes.

"What's the matter? Don't you like nature?"

Even though she knew he teased her, she still didn't like it. "I like nature as God intended. In a national park. Away from things that roar and can eat you."

He chuckled and took her hand again. She didn't object. As he headed through the foliage, he shoved gigantic leaves out of his way, which made them pop back in place, nearly hitting her in the face.

"Hey!" she snapped.

"Sorry."

To keep it from happening again, she held her free hand out in front of her.

As they made their way, something whizzed past his face, slicing the air between them. She peered into the brush from where it came when another and another sped by them. Dane shoved her to the ground, covering her with his body. Looking up, she saw a short spear lodged in the tree inches away from where she stood moments ago.

"I don't think we're in Kansas anymore," she whispered.

They could hear footsteps crashing through the

underbrush, heading in their direction. A sudden panic welled inside her as an unfriendly someone approached. She couldn't take much more of this.

"What are we going to do?" She tried to keep her voice normal, but it wavered a little in her panic.

"Shhh. Don't move."

How could she? He sprawled on top of her, not that she minded. Her heart throbbed painfully and her breathing increased to a rapid pace. She fought the urge to squirm out from under him, but she knew he would never allow her to move.

A voice queried a question. Masculine, thick with a strange accent, speaking what sounded like Spanish…but not quite Spanish.

A response she didn't understand followed. The other voice spoke in a hushed tone.

And then, appearing before them, was a darkly tanned foot wearing a leather sandal attached to a leg with colorful beads around the ankle. She craned her neck to look up at the man who seemed taller than any other human she had ever seen. He towered over them, his head blotting out the sun and his features indiscernible.

From what Skye could tell, a richly colored material of red and gold wrapped around his hips. A long sash in the same colors crossed his hairless chest and was tossed over his left shoulder. He held a long spear, strange medallions tied around the end at the point. He looked down at them, speaking in an unfamiliar tongue.

Another man prodded Dane in the back with a spear and barked an order in his native language.

"I think he wants you to get up," Skye said. "Even though I don't want you to."

Spear Man jabbed him again.

"Stay put," he ordered and got to his feet.

Sitting up, she watched Dane stand nose-to-nose with the native, his hands in a surrendering gesture. The second native pointed his spear in her face, and spoke rapidly and firmly.

"Uh, Dane, I think this guy wants me to get up, too."

"Right," he said through gritted teeth.

The native poked her in the shoulder with the pointy spear.

"Ow! That hurt."

She rose and propped her hands on her hips, glaring at the man.

She had been right. He towered over her. His dark face was painted with white and red lines around the eyes and down the cheeks. He wore golden armbands, wristbands, a golden choker around his throat, and a large golden earring in one ear that stretched out his lobe. His eyes went wide as he sucked in a sharp breath. He fell to his knees, bowing at her feet. The other native followed.

"What the hell...?" She trailed off.

"What are they doing?" Dane glanced between the two.

"I have no idea."

"This seems like a good sign," he said. "Maybe we can use it to our advantage."

"Maybe." She placed her hand on the stranger's shoulder, gave him a light pat.

He rose, bowed his head again, then spoke to his companion. The tall one reached for Skye's hair, fingered her coppery locks between his thumb and forefinger, looking at his companion and speaking at an excited rapid pace.

"Hey, no touchy." She pushed his hand away.

Why was it everywhere they ended up, the men had to touch her? Not knowing what else to call him, she mentally named this near-giant Tall Man.

Tall Man dropped his spear, put his palms together in a

prayer position and bowed to her, saying the same phrase over and over.

"*Perdoe-me, ta'rin da bara. Perdoe-me.*"

It seemed as though he asked for her forgiveness.

"All right, all right," Skye grumbled. "I wish I knew what they were saying."

"Yeah, me too," Dane concurred. "They think you're something special, though."

"Apparently."

Tall Man picked up his spear and he and his companion urged the two of them to follow. The natives headed through the underbrush. When Skye and Dane failed to go along, Tall Man turned again, speaking to them and waving for them to come.

"I guess he wants us to follow him, eh? Do you want to see where he leads us?"

"Why not," she replied.

It wasn't the weirdest thing that had happened all day, after all.

Don't miss any of Skye and Dane's Adventures!

Highland Fling, **Volume 1**

A girl, a hit man and a time machine may be more than Dane Fortune can handle.

"…characters with real chemistry and a rip-roaring adventure." —5 stars, Amazon Reviewer

"…a fun twist to time travel…" —4 stars, Amazon Reviewer

"Dane Fortune is a delicious blend of everything you want in a hero." —4 stars, BookBub Reviewer

"I liked the set up for this book. It's pretty exciting and I didn't want to put it down." —5 stars, Amazon Reviewer

Dead of Winter, **Volume 2**

At the mercy of a faulty time machine, will Skye and Dane be able to make it home alive?

"…heart-stopping…full of anxiety-inducing moments and nail-biting suspense." —5 stars, BookBub Reviewer

"…a fun adventure that will leave [you] wanting more Ransom and Fortune." —4 stars, Amazon Reviewer

"…you'll want book 1 first so you can join in the wild ride from the beginning." —5 stars, BookBub Reviewer

"Adding the element of time travel to a book already rife with fantastical events—the story's endless possibilities are spellbinding." —Fort Worth Magazine

The Citadel, Volume 3

Still lost in time, Skye and Dane face their most dangerous enemy yet.

"What an amazing and addicting series!" —5 stars, Amazon Reviewer

"... plenty of action and a great storyline kept me reading until I finished it!" —5 stars, Amazon Reviewer

"Can't wait for the next one!" —5 stars, Amazon Reviewer

Lord of the Underworld, Volume 4

This title has never been published before and is a brand new adventure!

"This was a fast paced read…" —4 stars, Amazon Reviewer

"…a fast paced time travel adventure that is such a fun and easy read." —5 stars, Amazon Reviewer

"…a well written story that kept me turning pages, I want to read the next book." —4 stars, BookBub Reviewer

Sword of Vengeance, Volume 5

Coming soon!

Praise for the Dragon Protectors

Desiring the Dragon Lord, Book 1

"Michelle Miles kicks off her new Dragon Protectors series with a bang…" —4 stars, Amazon Reviewer

"I read this book in just a couple of days. I couldn't put it down!" —5 stars, Amazon Reviewer

"…a wonderful book full of strong minded characters." —5 stars, Amazon Reviewer

Seducing the Dragon Knight, Book 2

"From the start this book has danger and a bit of mystery." —4 stars, Amazon Reviewer

"I love this author and this genre. A must read." —5 stars, Booksprout Reviewer

"I was half in love with Rafe when we met him in Desiring the Dragon Lord, but oh get me a fan and a cool drink, because his hot factor increased 100-fold in the second installment." —4 stars, Amazon Reviewer

Tempting Her Dragon Bodyguard, Book 3

"I loved reading this book and hope there are more to come." —5 stars, Amazon Reviewer

"Book three in the Dragon Protectors series a well written story that kept me turning pages. I had to know what was going to happen." —5 stars, Amazon Reviewer

"…a captivating storyline…" —4 stars, Amazon Reviewer

Praise for Age of Wizards

***In the Tower of the Wizard King,* Book 1**

"The book has a very strong and intriguing plotline as well as unforgettable characters. I liked the parallel narration of the present and the past as it made the story both more complicated and more involving…" —5 stars, Amazon Reviewer

"The mix of past and present stories brings the reader full circle and will keep you engrossed in the story. Beware though, you may not want to put the book down! …two thumbs up…!" —5 stars, Goodreads Reviewer

"Michelle Miles brilliantly weaves twists and turns, love stories both past and present, secrets, betrayal and revenge, with multi-dimensional characters, two different timelines and two different worlds." —5 stars, Amazon Reviewer

"I thoroughly enjoyed every aspect of this book, and highly recommend it. Filled with fantasy and three dimensional characters I couldn't put it down." —5 stars, Amazon Reviewer

***On the Hunt for the Wizard King,* Book 2**

"We really got to watch all of the characters grow and change throughout the book. No one was what you expected. Miles did a great job of keeping you guess and wondering what was around the next corner." —5 stars, Amazon Reviewer

"Wow! This story is so full of magic with action and adventure I could not put it down. The land of fae is an exciting magical world where anything can happen, and I definitely was not expecting some of the twist and turns that transpired." —5 stars, Amazon Reviewer

Also by Michelle Miles

Dream Walker
Call of the Dark

Age of Wizards
In the Tower of the Wizard King
On the Hunt for the Wizard King

A Ransom & Fortune Adventure
Highland Fling, Vol 1
Dead of Winter, Vol 2
The Citadel, Vol 3
Lord of the Underworld, Vol 4

Dragon Protectors
Desiring the Dragon Lord
Seducing the Dragon Knight
Tempting Her Dragon Bodyguard

Realm of Honor
One Knight Only
Only for a Knight
A Knight to Remember
A Knight Like No Other
Shadows of the Knight

Guardians of Atlantis
Tempting Eden
Seducing Eve
Ravishing Helene
Guardians of Atlantis Box Set

About the Author

Michelle Miles believes in fairy tales, true love and magic. She is the award-winning author of the epic fantasy, IN THE TOWER OF THE WIZARD KING, as well as the fantasy romance series, REALM OF HONOR, featuring knights and their ladies fair, and the paranormal dragon-shifter romance series, DRAGON PROTECTORS.

In her spare time, she enjoys listening to music, reading, cross-stitching and watching movies. Even though she's a native Texan, she loves castles, dragons, fairies and elves and is an avid Game of Thrones fan. She can be found online at Facebook, Twitter, Instagram, Pinterest, and Goodreads.

www.ingramcontent.com/pod-product-compliance
Lightning Source LLC
Chambersburg PA
CBHW071535100726
47908CB00004B/1405